The Battle Of The Conquerors

'Dipo Toby Alakija

ISBN: 978-978-49874-7-9
ISBN: 978-49874-7-3

Printed in United States

First published in 2012
Republished in 2016
by the publishing house of

CALVARY ROCK RESOURCES

19, Ajina Street, Ikenne Remo,
Ogun State,
Nigeria.

36, Thomson road
Gorton
Manchester
M18 7QQ
United Kingdom

270 Madison Avenue
Suite 1500, New York, NY 10016
United States

www.calvaryrock.org

<u>Dedication</u>
Dedicated to Christian soldiers and everybody that seeks to know nothing but the truth.

The Conqueror's Gate

There is a very narrow way
That seems so long and rough
Though it is the right way to go
For it leads to the Conquerors' Gate
Yet very few people go through the way

Enemies that are very determined
Lay siege to the Conquerors' Gate
Many people therefore opt for the shortcuts
Which seem to lead to the right way
Behold, it leads to the Loser's Gate

The Conquerors' Gate is for the violent
The weak people cannot break through
For the enemies lay in wait to kill
These with Conqueror's amour can pass
For the battle on the way is for Conquerors

The battle of the Conquerors can be fought
Only by those who are truly Conquerors
And who walks towards the Conqueror's Gate
When the Gate is opened for the Conquerors
It leads them to eternal bliss in Heaven.

PROLOGUE

WAKE UP, GIANT!
YOU ARE IN THE BATTLE FIELD.

I am Captain Concern in the Battle Of The Conquerors. I am dragged into the battle that began right after the creation of the earth the moment The Redeemer came into my life. By the virtue of my calling and service unto the Lord, I am duty bound to live and teach the truth in whichever way I can. Relating this story is one of the ways to wake up the sleeping giants and to remind everybody that we are all in the battlefield. Since we are yet to reach the place of rest, nobody is expected to feel comfortable in the battlefield. I therefore want you to see this story as a message that is sent to you by The Commander though Comforter. I am simply a vessel to deliver the message and nothing more to it.

Charles H. Spurgeon, one of the greatest people whose works and writings still bring spark into many lives including mine said:

"...We have in this age but few giants in grace who rise head and shoulder above the common height, men to lead us in deeds of heroism and efforts of unstaggering faith. After all, the work of Christian Church, though it must be done by all, often owes its being done to single individual of remarkable grace. The fact is, most of us are vastly inferior to the early Christians who, as I take it, were persecuted because they were thoroughly Christians, and we are not persecuted because we hardly are Christians at all. They were so earnest in the propagation of the redeemer's kingdom that they became the nuisance of the age in which they lived. They would not let error alone. They had not conceived the opinion that they were to hold the truth, and leave other people to hold error without trying to intrude their opinions upon them, but they preached Christ Jesus right and left, and delivered their testimonies against every sin..."

3

Every believer both - young and old, male and female has a battle to fight the moment he becomes a Christian. Satan who does not want anybody to believe in Christ declares war against anyone that becomes born-gain. He not only engages believers in battles but also uses everything that is available to him to keep people ignorant of their identities in Christ and makes them unmindful of their eternal destinations. In 2 Peter 3:1-8, the Bible says thus:

"This second epistle, beloved, I now write unto you; in both which I stir up your pure minds by way of remembrance:

"That ye may be mindful of the words which were spoken before by the holy prophets, and of the commandment of us the apostles of the Lord and Saviour:

"Knowing this first, that there shall come in the last days scoffers, walking after their own lusts,

"And saying, Where is the promise of his coming? for since the fathers fell asleep, all things continue as they were from the beginning of the creation.

"For this they willingly are ignorant of, that by the word of God the heavens were of old, and the earth standing out of the water and in the water:

"Whereby the world that then was, being overflowed with water, perished:

"But the heavens and the earth, which are now, by the same word are kept in store, reserved unto fire against the day of judgment and perdition of ungodly men.

"But, beloved, be not ignorant of this one thing, that one day is with the Lord as a thousand years, and a thousand years as one."

Satan has countless number of ways to keep people in perpetual bondage. He knows ways of drawing the hearts of men away from God and makes them cold or lukewarm. He knows the best way to attack Christians through the love of the world, lust of flesh, lust of the eyes and pride of life. Hence the word of God warns in 1 John 2:15-16:

"Love not the world, neither the things that are in the world. If any man love the world, the love of the Father is not in him.

"For all that is in the world, the lust of the flesh, and the lust of the eyes, and the pride of life, is not of the Father, but is of the world."

The war against believers is a spiritual one although the devil often times brings it into the physical realm through the use of fellow human beings and things of this world. But quite unfortunately, so many Christians are so ignorant of the battles around them that they constantly walk against the word of God. With so much proofs of the activities of the devil in the physical, spirit realms and the Scriptures, so many believers ignorantly and willfully give in to their enemy which the Bible describes in 1 Peter 5:8,

"...as a roaring lion, walketh about, seeking whom he may devour..."

Even though there are some giants of the Lord who are supposed to give helping hands to the weak in the battle, they have become weary and cold. They live in the past victories, forgetting the fact that as long as we are still in this world; the battle is not yet over. Are you one of the giants who are sleeping right in the battlefield? You need to be reminded that many have died in their slumber, many are wounded and quite a large number of people are recaptured by the devil all because they are ignorant of the battles they are involved in. Many are unaware of the power given to them and many did not even see the enemy at work despite what the Scriptures say. The real enemy of most Christians is not really the devil but ignorance of the enemy and his activities. Hence the Bible says in Hosea 4:6-9:

"My people are destroyed for lack of knowledge: because

thou hast rejected knowledge, I will also reject thee, that thou shalt be no priest to me: seeing thou hast forgotten the law of thy God, I will also forget thy children.

"As they were increased, so they sinned against me: therefore will I change their glory into shame.

"They eat up the sin of my people, and they set their heart on their iniquity.

"And there shall be, like people, like priest: and I will punish them for their ways, and reward them their doings."

As you are going to see in the story that is revealed to me as a message to both Christians and non-Christian, the enemy has a lot of powerful weapons and deadly messengers, which include Ignorance.

These enemies had defeated so many believers all round the world either by enticing them with things of this world or by making them to seek vanity instead of eternity. The Lord has assured them of the mansions in heaven but their enemy is always using their eyes to see and admire earthly mansions, which would be consumed with fire sooner or later. We are told in the Gospel according to Matthew 11:12,

"And from the days of John the Baptist until now the kingdom of heaven suffereth violence, and the violent take it by force."

But believers are not forceful in their belief. They call zealous people fanatics and call strong desire to serve and work with the Lord extremism. So many Christians of today had been lured back into the world through heresies, lust of the flesh, technology and disunity in the body of Christ. Many have missed the old path because it is not convenient. They have joined the jet age people who journey on the expressway rather than to walk on the narrow path.

As a giant of the Lord, if that is what you are, you have a duty to direct the people back to the word of God. If you are a modern day Christian, you are mandated to embrace the old time Christianity and stand against the standard of this world. If you are not a Christian at all, this is the time to become one. Why? It is because that is the only way you can have eternal life.

Being a Christian is more than the way people go about it. We are not only to live our lives in the standard of God but also warn non-Christians of impending danger that awaits them in hell. Christians must not watch as other people take risks of their eternal lives. They should be depressed that people are walking in the ways of destruction. Why? It is because Christians are going to account for the souls of those they have the privilege to share the Gospel with. The word of God gives the warning in Ezekiel 33:7-12,

"So thou, O son of man, I have set thee a watchman unto the house of Israel; therefore thou shalt hear the word at my mouth, and warn them from me.

"When I say unto the wicked, O wicked man, thou shalt surely die; if thou dost not speak to warn the wicked from his way, that wicked man shall die in his iniquity; but his blood will I require at thine hand.

"Nevertheless, if thou warn the wicked of his way to turn from it; if he do not turn from his way, he shall die in his iniquity; but thou hast delivered thy soul.

"Therefore, O thou son of man, speak unto the house of Israel; Thus ye speak, saying, If our transgressions and our sins be upon us, and we pine away in them, how should we then live?

"Say unto them, As I live, saith the Lord GOD, I have no pleasure in the death of the wicked; but that the wicked turn from his way and live: turn ye, turn ye from your evil ways; for why will ye die, O house of Israel?

"Therefore, thou son of man, say unto the children of thy people, The righteousness of the righteous shall not deliver him in the day of his transgression: as for the wickedness of the wicked, he shall not fall thereby in the day that he turneth from his wickedness; neither shall the righteous be able to live for his righteousness in the day that he sinneth."

The enemy of mankind, Satan is working seriously to ensure that people are either kept in bondage or made ignorant of the things around them. As God will not strike without first giving a warning, He is giving everybody the chance to repent and come to Him. As for those who have caught the revelation of what is happening, there is need to caution others. That is the essence of this story - to warn Christians, especially the cold and lukewarm believers and non-Christians that we are all in the battlefield. Everybody, including the strong ones can easily be defeated by his enemies if he is so ignorant or so self-depending or so confident in himself. The word of God warns in 1 Corinthians 10:12,

"Wherefore let him that thinketh he standeth take heed lest he fall."

The good news is that whatever is your level of Christian life - be it a child who just come to the knowledge of Christ or those who have attained the level of the servants of God, you have what it takes to overcome the enemy in the battle. The word of God gives us this assurance in 1 John 4:4,

"Ye are of God, little children, and have overcome them: because greater is he that is in you, than he that is in the world."
So no one has any reason to be defeated in the battle. And yet many are defeated because they choose not to be conquerors. The basis of this battle as established in 2 Timothy 2:4 is to please our Lord and Saviour. The passage says,

No man that warreth entangleth himself with the affairs of this life; that he may please him who hath chosen him to be a soldier.

A soldier is one who fights, not treasure hunter or one that seeks pleasure in the battlefield. As soldiers of Jesus Christ called

Conquerors, Christians are to fight and conquer forces, most of which cannot be seen, because we are all more than conquerors. The bible says in Romans 8:37-39,

Nay, in all these things we are more than conquerors through him that loved us.

For I am persuaded, that neither death, nor life, nor angels, nor principalities, nor powers, nor things present, nor things to come,

Nor height, nor depth, nor any other creature, shall be able to separate us from the love of God, which is in Christ Jesus our Lord."

Are you a conqueror? Time will tell who the conqueror is.

CHAPTER ONE

There is a kingdom called Bondage and the king is called Wickedness. Wickedness has three various levels of great warriors who had been fighting the people since he took over the kingdom from the real rulers called First Couple.

The category of warriors in the first level is called Principalities. These warriors largely fight the slaves in the Flesh though they are also effective in other battlefields. The warriors in the second level are called Powers. While they are a little superior to the first level, they are somewhat inferior to the ones in the third level. The third level warriors which are next to Wickedness in authority and superiority are called Rulers of Darkness.

Wickedness through Serpent used a deadly weapon called Deception to take over the kingdom soon after First Couple was given dominion over the place. Serpent who worked with two other warriors called Lust Of The Eyes and Seditions before they could overthrow First Couple came as friendly neighbours. The kingdom was first called Garden. It was actually established by the Supreme Being called The Father who dwells in the place called Eternity. First Couple whose children later became slaves of Wickedness inhabited Garden. When Wickedness took over the government of Garden, he turned the place into Bondage; the kingdom that is now characterized with pains, sorrows, hardships and much sufferings.

The names of most of the warriors in all the levels that make

Bondage a terrible place to dwell are Ignorance, Pride, Lust Of The Eyes, Lust Of The Flesh, Adultery, Fornication, Uncleanness, Lasciviousness, Idolatry, Witchcraft, Hatred, Variance, Emulation, Wrath, Strife, Sedition, Heresies, Envying, Murders, Drunkenness, Ravelling, Fear In Various Forms, Unbelief, Doubt and Lies.

These warriors made all the subjects of the kingdom degenerated species. The people toiled from day to day from the time they are born up to the time they would go into the grave. The Father who loves the people becomes very sorrowful at the way Wickedness is ruling them but there is hardly anything he could do about the kingdom since First Couple had legally given it away. He, however, decides to send his only begotten son, The Redeemer who is an heir to the throne in Eternity to redeem the people from slavery before he destroys Bondage with fire. He has created a place called Doom, a place that burns with fire and brimstone where Wickedness and his warriors would be locked up on the judgment day. Wickedness knows this. So he determines to take as many slaves as possible with him. He seems to be making a huge success until The Father sent The Redeemer to Bondage.

The Redeemer is so powerful that his name alone can defeat Wickedness and all his warriors put together. He is also so humble that he took the form of one of the slaves in the kingdom so that he could help the people in Bondage to escape to Eternity where there is no pain, no sorrow - nothing but bliss. Although The Redeemer is a wonderful and powerful king of kings but when he got to Bondage, he was not recognized at first because he did not look like someone who could redeem the slaves from Wickedness. Of course, the warriors know that The Redeemer has come to save the people from them. So they sent warriors called Hatred and Confusion to turn the people against The Redeemer. Hatred and Confusion made the people to disbelieve The Redeemer as their saviour. They made the people wonder how someone who claimed to be their messiah to come in form of a slave. Even though the message of truth, which he had brought, was meant to liberate them from Wickedness, only few slaves believed in him and

11

became free from the torments of the warriors of king Wickedness. Ignorance aided Hatred and Confusion in making most of the slaves shun the message of freedom from slavery. Many of them do not even believe they are slaves, let alone to accept the offer to be redeemed. At first, twelve of them believed The Redeemer. Then hundreds and then thousands believed. The people that were set free made The Redeemer their king and saviour. But as soon as the warriors of king Wickedness heard of it, Lies came against him with Falsehood, took him before a minor king in one village in the kingdom where his body was later marred with stripes. Some of the slaves put a crown of thorns on his head; trying to make him appeared like a criminal. He was hanged on the tree and killed at last. Right inside the grave, The Redeemer continued to fight for the people until the third day. He rose up from the grave three day later to prove to the people that he is too powerful to be kept in the grave. When he arose, a lot of people began to realize that the messiah have actually come for them.

The Redeemer gathered his followers and said, "I am the good shepherd; the good shepherd gives his life for the sheep... Come unto me, you that labour and are heavy laden and I will give you rest … Come out of Bondage. Do not touch unclean thing for I will make you a chosen generation, a royal priesthood, a holy nation, a peculiar people that will show the praises of Him who had called you out of darkness unto his marvelous light.'

The people soon formed a family that later grew into many families. The families later grew so big that they formed many members of one huge body called Congregations. The Redeemer heads all the Congregations. He uses another Supreme Being called Comforter to direct all the activities of the people. Comforter, just like The Father and The Redeemer, is from Eternity. For the first time in their lives, the people who were once slaves experienced real joy. The Redeemer treats his followers with great love and care. He is merciful and gracious, slow to anger and plenteous in mercy. He provides them with everything they need and protects them against the warriors of King Wickedness. Then the people begin to sing:

Bless the LORD, O my soul: and all that is within me, bless his holy name.

Bless the LORD, O my soul, and forget not all his benefits:

Who forgiveth all thine iniquities; who healeth all thy diseases;

Who redeemeth thy life from destruction; who crowneth thee with lovingkindness and tender mercies;

Who satisfieth thy mouth with good things; so that thy youth is renewed like the eagle's.

The Redeemer is glad to note that the people love him so dearly. He looks at them with compassion for they are like sheep without a Shepherd. To add more to his sorrow, he could not take his mind away from those in the land of Bondage. Two big tears roll from his eyes.

The people look agitated and ask, "oh, Lord, the King, what is the matter?"

The Redeemer says, "I have pleasure in you all but I do not have pleasure in the deaths of any of the other slaves in Bondage."

"Well then," the people say, "we'll go into the kingdom and tell everybody about you and the benefits we have enjoyed so far."

"That's very good," The Redeemer says. "Verily, verily, I say unto you, He that heareth my word, and believeth on him that sent me, hath everlasting life, and shall not come into condemnation; but is passed from death unto life. Go ye therefore into all the nooks and crannies of the kingdom and tell them the good news."

And so the people go into the kingdom to tell the rest of the slaves about The Redeemer and his kingdom in Eternity. Many people soon begin to leave Bondage to join the redeemed people in Congregations. Before Wickedness and his warriors got to know about it, many people had been won over to The Redeemer.

Wickedness becomes furious at everybody in Bondage. The

13

words of The Redeemer ring in the mouth of his followers, "woe to the inhabiters of Bondage and of the sea! for Wickedness is come down unto you, having great wrath, because he knoweth that he hath but a short time."

Truly, Wickedness knows his destruction and that of his warriors is close by. He knows furthermore that his kingdom is at stake, most especially when the heir of Eternity is making the slaves to leave his kingdom and turning them into his enemies. He would have loved to deal with The Redeemer once and for all for coming to redeem the slaves from him but he knows he is no match for him. So trying to get hold of him or any of his followers is out of question. There is only one way to solve the problem. He would make as many slaves as possible to stay away from The Redeemer and his followers. Through that, he could be assured that most of the slaves will go down with him to Doom. If he makes best use of his warriors and his deadly weapons, he would not only keep the slaves but also the kingdom of Bondage. Though The Father would sooner or later destroy the kingdom with fire, he could still keep it as his property for a while and the slaves for eternity. He hopes to use his valuable warrior, Ignorance who can make the rest of the slaves unaware of whom The Redeemer is. Apart from that, he would send the dreadful looking warrior called Fear In Various Forms to send threats of instant death to anybody that mentions the name of The Redeemer, let alone to follow him. Actually, Fear has no power or means to carry out any of the threats but the warrior has a very effective way of making the slaves to follow orders of Wickedness. All he has to do is to roar as loud as he can or create unreal circumstances that are threatening enough. Although this trick rarely works on true Conquerors, because they know through the words that greater is he that is with them than anything that is in Bondage, yet he often times succeeds with those who do not know how powerful the name of The Redeemer is. Many of the followers understand that death is actually the messenger of The Father called Eternal Rest. He is to take the Conquerors from Bondage to Eternity where they will reign with The Redeemer. So they are not always intimidated even if they are faced with the circumstances that threaten their lives. Only the followers who are unaware of whom The Redeemer is and where he is taking them to are usually intimidated by Fear In Various Forms. It is the duty of Ignorance to hide the fact that the death of a Conqueror is actually a vehicle called Eternal Rest, which is to take him to Eternity. The warriors are to make death looks frightening and horrible, especially to many redeemed people who lack the understanding about the teachings of their Lord and Saviour. By sending Fear In Various Forms and Ignorance out with the first batch of warriors for the people to contend with, Wickedness hopes to keep as many slaves as possible and to make the Conquerors ineffective in their efforts to set them free.

King Wickedness sends other warriors like Persecutions round the kingdom to warn the people that anybody that is found listening or talking about The Redeemer shall be put to death. Many Conquerors who go about sharing the good news are faced with deaths in various ways but they know better than to give up. To them, it is better to let deaths be the vehicles that would take them to Eternity where they would have everlasting rest and joy than to allow the slaves to end up in Doom. Seeing that deaths have taken many of the followers away, the warriors of king Wickedness are encouraged, thinking that they could get others so easily. Wickedness sees their deaths as evidence to prove to the slaves that his warriors could get the followers without problems. This, of course, makes many slaves too afraid to follow The Redeemer.

Wickedness enlists more warriors to fight both the slaves that are becoming unruly and the Conquerors at every nook and cranny of the kingdom. Not quite long, King Wickedness and his warriors formally declare war against the redeemed people. He has the confidence that he would win the war because the people are not equipped or trained to fight.

The Redeemer gathers the people at Congregations, which are made up of mostly women, some with suckling children, some with husbands; some are singles, some whose spouses are dead or living in Bondage. They are of various ages and status.

15

Wickedness and his warriors laugh at them because they could not imagine how such frail looking people would fight with him and his warriors who have several thousands of years of experiences in the war. The condition of everybody in each Congregation seems so pathetic but their faith in The Redeemer is so strong that their faces glow with hope and burning desire to please their Lord. They all seem ready to die for The Redeemer because they know they are always in his heart.

"Wickedness has declared war against you," The Redeemer says, looking at the people. "But the battle is not for you. It is for me. I shall fight for you and you shall hold your peace... Let not your heart be troubled, you believe in my Father and me... In my Father's house there are many mansions. If it were not so, I would have told you. I go to prepare a place for you in Eternity and I will come again to receive you unto myself, so that where I am, there you may be also... When we get to Eternity, I will wipe away all tears from your eyes and there shall be no more death, neither sorrow, nor crying neither shall there be any more pains. For the former things shall pass away." He pauses to look around at the people. They are all very attentive. "I must warn you about Wickedness and his kingdom. My father has appointed a time when Bondage will be burnt with fire. All the people including Wickedness and his servants will be thrown into a lake, which burns with fire and brimstone. So it is very important for you to warn everybody in Bondage to come to me. I am the only way out of the danger that is awaiting all the people in Bondage. I must not fail to warn you also that you're going to face a lot of problems when I am gone. From henceforth, there shall be five in one house divided, three against two and two against three. Don't think my presence in the land of Bondage will bring peace. No! In fact, a man's foes shall be they of his own household. You shall be seriously persecuted for my sake but be of good cheers for I have overcome the enemies. Set your minds on things, which I am going to prepare for you in Eternity. Fear not the one who can only kill your body and can do nothing to the soul but fear he that is able to burn in the lake of fire. Seek ye not what ye shall eat or drink but

16

let everybody seek the kingdom of The Father and how to get there. As from now on, the kingdom of The Father had become violent to enter because Wickedness will try to stop you from getting to the place at every side. Therefore, it is not enough to stand and think you will enter. You must fight your own way into Eternity. I am going to give you just two things before I go. The two things are the whole armour of The Father. You must not underrate Wickedness. He is a powerful and cunning warrior. You can never defeat him without this armour. You must always put it on till I come. Without it, you can never face Wickedness and his warriors in the battle. Both young and old must wear it everyday. If anyone of it is missing, Wickedness or his warriors can get you down. If he gets you down, he will throw you inside bottomless pit, which will take you to the place called Doom. Doom is the lake of fire that is actually prepared for Wickedness and his messengers. You must teach your children how to use it and teach those who are coming to join you in the Congregations. Secondly, I will give Comforter to you. He is the Spirit of truth who will come from The Father in Eternity. He shall teach and guide you in all the things about your new life as citizens of Eternity. Through him you shall know many things, including the mysteries about Eternity and you shall be my witnesses in the land of Bondage. He will give you the boldness to tell people about me. He will give you the power and the authority over all your enemies, including Wickedness. You must listen and obey him. You must not grieve him or seek after things in the land of Bondage. I will be the one to supply you all you need, including your daily bread. You must not seek those things, which the people in Bondage seek after. Behold, I give you power to tread on serpents and scorpions, and over all the power of the enemy: and nothing shall by any means hurt you. Go your ways: behold I send you as lambs among wolves. Carry neither purse, nor scrip, nor shoes. Since you are set free, not through your own efforts, you must seek therefore the freedom of others by telling the people about good news. You must always say, 'the kingdom of Eternity is open to everybody. Come, forsake all your activities and be redeemed.' Do not fear even if the earth be removed, and though the mountain is carried into the midst of the sea. Lo! Through Comforter, I will be with you always!"

Having got so much courage and assurance from The Redeemer, his people begin to prepare to go into war with Wickedness, putting on the whole armour he had given to each of them.

CHAPTER TWO

Soon, news reached Wickedness through the messengers he had placed to spy on The Redeemer that his people are all putting on the of armours of war. He knows he and his warriors are in for a big trouble. So he called an emergency meeting with the warriors. They must to do something about the armour before it is too late. No one seemed to know the implications of the armour except Wickedness. All others thought that they could easily disarm the people of the armour since they are not even trained soldiers. Besides, the warriors had been fighting the battle from generation to generation. So, definitely, the people are no match for them; no matter how effective their armours.

Wickedness looked worried as he gazed mindlessly at the warriors who were waiting for his order to begin to attack and strike the Conquerors. "Do you know that we can never strike the Conquerors without casualties as long as they are putting on the whole amour?" he asked them.

The warriors exchanged glances, asking in diverse ways, "why not?"

"The armour is not ordinary armour," Wickedness explained. "Any fool would be able to use the armour effectively if he follows the simple instruction The Redeemer gives to them." He paused, looking very passive. "Let me explain the implications of the whole armour to you. It will make it extremely difficult, if not impossible, for us to use any of the weapons we have hoped to attack the people with. The loins of the people are guarded with truth, making it impossible for powerful warriors like Deceit, Falsehood or Lies to operate.

"The breastplate will make it impossible for Accusations, Hypocrisy, Scandal and so many other warriors to attack them with their weapons and tricks. The breastplate is the armour that guide against arrows of these warriors from reaching them. For the armour to be effective, however, each of the Conquerors needs to wear underwear that is made with white material. It is designed by Righteousness, one of the soldiers of Comforter. They Conquerors must always put on the underwear before they can be victorious with the use of the entire armour. It is a perquisite and must always be kept clean. If it is made dirty, it must be washed with what is called The Blood. Any follower of The Redeemer that put on dirty underwear would smell like shit. Comforter who needs to help them use the armour cannot stand dirty things or bad odour without being grieved. So it is duty of Uncleanness to make the followers smell like shit. Mind you, once they are purified again with The Blood, we would have to find a place to hide because they'd be back on their feet with full force.

"Their feet are covered with shoes that are marked with the preparation of the word of The Redeemer. Therefore, they have the power to walk anywhere they like and tell the slaves about The Redeemer. We really can't afford to let them go around here telling the slaves about The Redeemer. If they get to know that The Redeemer is their messiah, they will become his followers. The implication of that is that we will have more and more followers that will engage us in the fight. I don't need to tell you how dangerous that is. Having to contend with the Conquerors with their dangerous weapons is more than enough to cause us a major disaster. Having more slaves to join them to war against us spells much more calamity. If at all we fail to get back the Conquerors as our slaves, we must not fail to prevent them from getting our slaves. Weariness and Discouragement have the duty to stop them from going far. With what The Redeemer has given them so far, if we are not careful, the number of followers we have as enemies are more than enough to level our kingdom without sweat. I can never over emphasis that fact. So preventing more slaves to become followers is one of the main reasons we must fight to the finish."

He paused to look at the warriors again. He continued after a moment, "the shield is made by two of the mysterious soldiers of Comforter called Faith and Patience. The shield is what the people can use to quench all our fiery darts like sickness, weakness, affliction, tribulation, distress, persecution, famine, nakedness, peril and sword which we hope to use against them. Without the shield, they will have nothing that can defend them against the darts.

"The helmet of salvation is the symbol of freedom and citizenship of Eternity. You know that Eternity is enough reason for any right thinking person to become the follower of The Redeemer. It is a joyful place to be. We were once there, remember? I hate to think of how we missed the place and I hate the idea of The Redeemer taking his followers to the place while we live in torments and agonies in Doom. Well, we'll see to it that most of the people do not get there. We are going to make the place so difficult to enter that only violent people will get in. To get in, it must be by war and by force. Let's do all we can to remove the real helmet and give them the counterfeit, which we shall design. If they wear the counterfeit helmet, they may claim to be Conquerors but in reality, they would remain our slaves who are controlled by one of our warriors called Religion.

"The most dangerous of all the armours is the sword of the Spirit which is made with the words of The Redeemer. To use this sword against us, all the people need to do is to raise their shield and say the word. In order words, the followers can command any situation with the words of The Redeemer. Needless to say, the people can get victories for themselves with the words of their mouths." He paused to study the reactions of the warriors.

The warriors were as terrified as he expected.

"You don't have to look as if you are in shock!" Wickedness roared at them. "Just because they have the power to terrorize us does not mean they can deal with us. Negative Confessions, Curses, Self Pity and a host of other warriors like that can make them use the weapons against themselves through what they say."

He paused to look round at them again. They were yet to recover from the first shock. "And then," he continued after a while as if he had not terrified them enough, "'there is this being called Comforter. It is through him that The Redeemer can keep an eye on each of his followers. Comforter is not an ordinary being. He is always accompanied with mysterious soldiers like Love, Boldness, Knowledge Of The Word, Wisdom, Grace and Joy among so many other super powerful soldiers. Knowledge Of The Word empowers the people and reveals all our secrets to them. Wisdom teaches them how to foil our strategies. Only Ignorance can tackle Knowledge. Grace and Joy give the people in the battle unusual strength, no matter how weak the followers may be. As long as Grace and Joy are with the followers, they can never be weary. Love, on the other hand, speaks the language that is understood by everybody, including children. When Love speaks, people listen and obey him. Love is instantly trusted when he operates. Love endures a lot. He is kind. He can defeat so many warriors at a go. The combinations of forces of warriors like Envy, Pride, Provocations, Evil Thoughts, Hopelessness, Imaginations, Variance, Hatred, Failures and so many others like that are no match for him alone. What gives Love so much strength is the ability to speak all the languages like Forgiveness, Appreciations, Caring Attitudes, Selflessness, Sacrifice, Kind Words, Tenderness, Compassion, Affectionate feelings, Smiles, Helping Hands, Laying Down Life, Encouragements, and Cheerfulness. When Love smiles at people, they do anything to possess him.

"If just one of the mysterious soldiers is as powerful as that, you can imagine the havoc a follower of The Redeemer who is always in the company of Comforter can wreck in our kingdom. The Redeemer knows how important Comforter is to his followers. He will not only guide them on how to be effective with the use of armour but also teach them all things, including how to foil our strategies and render our weapons useless. With what The

Redeemer has given his followers so far, they all have all the chances to defeat us without efforts. With the use of the powerful armour and with the help of Comforter and soldiers, the smallest among the Conquerors is big enough to tackle our combined forces."

The warriors were stunned the more. Wickedness too could not hide his confusion and frustrations as he thought of the strength The Redeemer has given to his followers. He did not know why he has to go that far. It was enough to rescue the slaves from him. He should have left it like that.

There was uncomfortable silence. Every one of them really needed a very good reason they should get involved in a battle that spelt disaster for them.

"Why does The Redeemer give the people so much power that could be used to terrorize us?" Variance asked angrily and suddenly.

Wickedness' voice did not sound like his as he said, "it was Love that made him go that far! We really have to tackle that soldier."

"How can we possibly do that? It looks impossible to defeat the Conquerors in the battle." Witchcraft said, breaking the long uncomfortable silence. "Since the armour is powerful enough to get the followers victories and since Comforter is always around to help them, what's our chance of victory? To me, it's like we are fighting the battle we have already lost. Moving any close to the people is like digging our own graves with our own hands."

Wickedness, sitting on his throne smiled. Witchcraft was dead right but she was ignorant of many things. If only she knew there was always a way to defeat the people, she would not talk like a fool. In fact, they were at the meeting to think of how to deal with them, not just to analyze the strengths of the Conquerors. "Well," he said in a very passive mood, 'I have not called you here to make you feel that the situation is hopeless. I have called you rather to let you see the strengths of the enemies we are dealing with and to see how we can defeat them."

"If you ask me how, I'll say I can't see the possibility of

defeating such people. They are obviously too strong for us to handle, going by your explanations," Variance said. "Like Witchcraft pointed out, it is a suicide mission if we try to get close to them. With Comforter and his mysterious armies around the people who are putting on that kind of deadly armour, we don't stand a chance to defeat the people!"

"That's true!" the other warriors agreed.

"I can assure you that it is not a suicide mission," Wickedness said. "The Conquerors are very strong. No doubt about that. In fact a follower is a potential conqueror. But you all understand that it is not enough to be strong to win in the battle. There are other essential things that are required in a good warrior. I think we have some advantages over them in these areas."

"What are those advantages?" Strife asked quickly and eagerly. He wanted to be the first to take the advantage.

Wickedness smiled at him. He loves zealous warriors. Strife is one of the most zealous warriors that are ready to take any chance to strike their enemies, no matter how little the chance may be. He does that to impress others or to prove that he is the best warrior. Whatever the reason for always proving that he is so good is immaterial to Wickedness. All he wants is effective and efficient warrior. "The chance we have over the people," Wickedness said after a brief silence, "is that the redeemed people; like I told you; must wear clean garment that is made by one of the soldiers of Comforter called Righteousness before they can be effective with the use of the armour. Anyone that wears it is practically invulnerable. If the garment is either dirty or removed, it makes them vulnerable and almost defenseless. Armour like the breastplate would be missing, making a follower vulnerable to any of our darts. As you know, the darts can easily weaken them."

"What if Grace and Joy are with the follower to strengthen him if they are weakened?" Lust Of The Flesh asked.

"That's a very good question. Again as I told you earlier, without clean underwear that is required to put on the armours, Comforter would not be able to relate or help them use them. The relationship of a follower with Comforter is so crucial that everything, including their lives and victories depends on it. Though Comforter will tell the followers through one way or the other what they need to do, he will never enforce his will over them. Though he is so powerful that his presence in the life of a follower can cause a disaster in our kingdom, he is so mild that a follower that is so occupied can hardly hear him. If we take the garments of Righteousness from the followers or make them dirty, the relationship between them and Comforter can be broken easily. Through that alone, we can practically disarm the follower without much problem."

"How can you be so sure?" Fear asked.

"If you study the words of The Redeemer carefully, you'll get all these facts," Wickedness replied with assurance. "With what I know about The Redeemer, he doesn't go or do things against his words. Unlike us who have the privilege to deceive and manipulate anybody as we like, he does not have that chance. The only thing that is impossible for him to do is to lie or change his words. He's always bound by his words. In any case, he speaks the truth because he is the truth, the way to The Father and the life in Eternity. So we can count on all what he tells his people as the truth."

"There other deadly weapons like the sword," Doubt said. "If the people use that against us, we'll still feel sorry for getting close to them."

"You are not listening to me, Doubt, are you? I said Negative Confessions and Curses could make the followers to destroy themselves with the weapons. Besides that, the effective use of the whole armour depends largely on the relationship of the people with Comforter. Without Comforter, the entire armour will be very burdensome for them. In fact, they can never put them on without his help, let alone to use them against us. So the garment of Righteousness is crucial for them to get victories. In order to have and retain this garment, The Redeemer gives the followers the rules they must follow. These rules are his words. If they follow his words, they will live a victorious life. The words serve as conditions and standard to retain this garment. If they do not meet

25

up to the standard, Comforter will be grieved. If he is grieved, he will leave them. If he leaves them, they'll not be different from our slaves. One of the strategies we must employ in this battle is the focus of our efforts at removing their garments of Righteousness or staining them by making them break the rules. Each of you must come up with at least a tactic that will make them remove or stain the garments. For instance, Ignorance can hide the words of The Redeemer from the redeemed people. If they are fighting us without the words, they will lose without rules."

"What if Knowledge Of The Word tackles Ignorance?" Strife asked. He really did not like any warriors appearing more relevant than him.

"Well, you are there to help. Other warriors like Pride, Holier-Than-Thou, Self Righteous and a host of others are there to attack them if they escape from Ignorance. The fact is: most of the people do not know that their victories depend so much on their relationship with Comforter and how much they follow these rules. We can rightly say that as powerful as they seem, they can be destroyed easily through their inability to understand the source of their strengths. More so, they just start to war. We've been fighting wars for thousands of years. So we are much more trained and equipped with a lot of tricks and wisdom than the people. We have enough information about each of the followers. They have no knowledge of the methods we are going to use to fight them. We all know that most of the people, if not at all of them, love pleasures. Many of them, therefore, will be willing to trade their armour of war with pleasures since they do not know the value. You know, once we take the armour from them, they are dead. Beside that, one of our greatest weapons against the people is their inability to appreciate the power in the words The Redeemer has given to them. Since they don't appreciate the power, the warrior called Fear In Various Forms with his team has the duty to roar like lions and give them the evidence of things that appear so real. This will naturally weaken and cause them to flee. Once they flee, they will turn back from the war. As you know that the armour is not designed to cover the backs of the redeemed people, we can easily shoot fiery darts at the backslider and make his life more miserable than when he was our slave."

Suddenly the whole place was filled with uproar of joy. Everybody hailed Wickedness for his brilliant idea. His idea spurred more ideas among the warriors.

"What you said gave me another idea," Pride said. "I can cause the heart of the people to be lifted up after little achievement. Once I fill their hearts, they will lose focus. Once they lose their focus in the battle, we can easily disarm them. Apart from this, my lord, I can design other garments that look nice and clean with a team of my friends called Titles, High Positions, Superiority, High Minds, Arrogance, Egotism, Haughtiness, Conceit, Self-Importance and a host of others. We'll distribute the garments among the people and persuade them to put them on instead of wearing the garments of Righteousness that make them look so common, cheap and inferior to others."

"Good of you!" Wickedness cheered. He intended to encourage others to bring in their ideas.

"I have an idea too," Lust Of The Eye said excitedly. "I've used it before and it worked like magic."

"Let's hear it," Wickedness said enthusiastically.

"First Couple fell for my trick. I used the eyes of the woman to look at the forbidden fruits, which they were not supposed to eat. I said, 'you can see that the fruit is beautiful to eat, can't you?' the woman agreed with me and ate the forbidden fruit, which made her and her husband to lose this kingdom to us. I can use the same old trick and cause the people to neglect the things The Redeemer promised them in Eternity. I will let them see the beautiful things around which they stand to gain if they remove the armour of war. Once they remove the armour, they'll be dead!"

"Beautiful!" Wickedness cheered. The rest clapped for Lust Of The Eye for the brilliant idea. Lust Of The Flesh too stood up and said, "I think I can also deal with them too through the desires of their flesh. I expect you to count on me when you were thinking of making the people to put down their armour of war through pleasures. Anyway, I will use weapons like sexual gratification and love of money to remove the garments of Righteousness and break the relationship between them and Comforter. Once that is done, they will remove the armour by themselves and once they remove it, we'll bounce on them and butcher them."

"That's another good one," Wickedness said.

"I can deal with them too," Adultery said. "I will use weapons like extra marital sex and temptations to fight the people. All I need before I strike a deadly blow against the follower is just an opportunity to make a married person to lay with someone who is not his or her spouse. And, as you know, there is no way they can do that without removing the garment of Righteousness. Once they remove it, we'll simply squeeze life out of them."

"That's also another good idea," Wickedness said. As far as he is concerned, all ideas are good as long as they are directed at removing the armour from the redeemed people.

Fornication stood up and said, "I'll not be left behind in the work too. I will lead the people captive through sexual immoralities, especially among the youths. I will make use of weapon like premarital-sex and temptations to fight the people also. My activities just like that of Adultery will not only open doors for so many other warriors to strike them but also to tear their garments of Righteousness into pieces. I will focus much of my attention on the young followers. I will use beauty, indecent dressing and other weapons to tear the garments of as many people as I can. You know, once I can get the garment out of their bodies, all we'll have are their corpses. They will be dead before they know it."

"Good, good of you," Wickedness said.

Uncleanness stood up and said thoughtfully, "let me see what I can do ... Oh yes, I get it now. You all remember what I did in the Congregation in Thyatira where I used one of our slaves called Jezebel to bring abominable acts into the congregation. The people thought she was a prophetess. Before anybody got to know that I was using her to bring the abominable acts into the Congregation, the entire members were neck deep inside dirty things that made their garments look like shit. I can use the same old trick. You can bet it with me that I'll succeed."

"I know you will succeed, Uncleanness," Wickedness said. "I can testify to that. You can work on your plans very well. We really count on you to wreck a lot of havoc in the Congregations of the redeemed people with a lot of shit, filth, mud - anything."

"Yes, I know. I'll push as many people as possible into the mud and filth. I promise you I'll not fail you."

Wickedness waved at Lasciviousness who looked as if he has something to say.

Lasciviousness cleared his throat and said, "you've all been talking now. I'm sure you expected me to come up with an idea too. Well, I think I am indispensable. I can deal with the people too in such an uncommon way. I'll use weapons like late-marriage or delayed-marriage against the strong and matured Conquerors. I'll also use a weapon like uncontrolled-sexual urge and pornography to fight against the youths that are full of energy. Instead of fighting war with us, I'll cause them to lust after one another like street dogs. With my big plan, I will make the redeemed people to throw their garments of Righteousness into the rubbish dump. In fact, I'll make them consider the garment as old fashion stuff that must be replaced with nudity. We'll have fun fighting them in the nude. It'll be spectacular show as we make mess of their bodies."

"Good, good of you; Lasciviousness!'" Wickedness said excitedly.

Idolatry stood up and said, "now, now, I'm going to say something that'll prove to you that I'm a very useful warrior too. A lot of people think I'm going to use the same old idea of worshiping idols. I'm sure many of the people would not fall for that stuff again because we are in the new age. The new trick I have designed now is much more sophisticated and complicated. I'm going to fill the hearts of the people with the idea of making money by all means and direct their attention to material things. I will entice the people to pursue those things every day of their lives instead of things that pertain to Eternity. In the cause of doing that, they will break so many rules and lower the standard The Redeemer has set for them.

I will replace the love of their Lord with love of those things. That's not all. I will use what the people cherish most as weapons or idols that will occupy their hearts. With my great plans, there will be no space or time for them to think or talk about The Redeemer and Eternity. They'll worship money, human beings like them and even their bellies instead of fighting battles with us."

"That's very brilliant of you, idolatry;" Wickedness said.

Witchcraft did not want the rest to feel she was an idiot who has no idea to offer. She stood up and said, "alright, I think I know exactly what to do now. This is the way I'm going to fight against the Conquerors. I will use the gifts, the skills and talents of some of our slaves as weapons to bewitch and hypnotize the people. They would be filled with various ideas that are contrary to the words of The Redeemer. I will introduce all kinds of things to influence their thinking. Such things may take the forms of entertainment, education and information. I will establish and organize associations, political activities, public concerts and even lectures where the people would be influenced to go against the words. Through my activities, I can burn their garments of Righteousness and give them with the ones that are made by Unrighteousness. Of course, I will make them feel that they are putting on the real ones. I can even use a weapon like magic to make them feel their garments are real ones. I can go as far as making so many others to forget about Eternity. I will convince many of the people that The Redeemer means nothing to them and he is no longer coming back to take them to Eternity as he has promised them. Even if some continue to believe there is a place called Eternity, I will work with warriors like Religions and Heresies to introduce the people to ways that seem to be the right way to Eternity. In fact, I am capable of appearing like The Redeemer and fool the people. Besides, I can initiate the people that are seeking for knowledge or powers through lectures, books, meetings, personal contact and even through dreams into the kingdom of powers and principalities. I will use the initiated people to fight the redeemed people. I will give the initiated people wisdom to spread lies about The Redeemer and pervert his words. Guess what! These people will

30

also use a weapon like uncontrolled-sexual urge and pornography to fight against the youths that are full of energy. Instead of fighting war with us, I'll cause them to lust after one another like street dogs. With my big plan, I will make the redeemed people to throw their garments of Righteousness into the rubbish dump. In fact, I'll make them consider the garment as old fashion stuff that must be replaced with nudity. We'll have fun fighting them in the nude. It'll be spectacular show as we make mess of their bodies."

"Good, good of you; Lasciviousness!'" Wickedness said excitedly.

Idolatry stood up and said, "now, now, I'm going to say something that'll prove to you that I'm a very useful warrior too. A lot of people think I'm going to use the same old idea of worshiping idols. I'm sure many of the people would not fall for that stuff again because we are in the new age. The new trick I have designed now is much more sophisticated and complicated. I'm going to fill the hearts of the people with the idea of making money by all means and direct their attention to material things. I will entice the people to pursue those things every day of their lives instead of things that pertain to Eternity. In the cause of doing that, they will break so many rules and lower the standard The Redeemer has set for them. I will replace the love of their Lord with love of those things. That's not all. I will use what the people cherish most as weapons or idols that will occupy their hearts. With my great plans, there will be no space or time for them to think or talk about The Redeemer and Eternity. They'll worship money, human beings like them and even their bellies instead of fighting battles with us."

"That's very brilliant of you, idolatry;" Wickedness said.

Witchcraft did not want the rest to feel she was an idiot who has no idea to offer. She stood up and said, "alright, I think I know exactly what to do now. This is the way I'm going to fight against not even know that they are serving us. If you think that's all, you're wrong. I will initiate people, including the children through their friends, schools and even through what they read and eat. My operation is so unlimited that I can spread my activities to all nooks and crannies of the kingdom within a very short time. With my strategy, I can make it difficult for the words of The Redeemer to reach the people."

"Beautiful!" Wickedness said excitedly, green with joy.

"I'm not through yet," Witchcraft said, hoping to impress him the more.

"I understand everything in a flash," Wickedness said. "You don't need to give me the details. All I want you to do is to work on your strategy very well. In the next meeting, you'll share the details with us. The same thing is applicable to every other warrior."

He looked at the rest of the warriors who were yet to come up with their ideas and said, "all of you must come up with ideas now."

CHAPTER THREE

The meeting continued in the palace of King Wickedness with profound consideration to the potentials of the enemies of their kingdom the redeemed people. With what had been said so far, the warriors of Wickedness could sense that the Conquerors were much more powerful than their combined forces but they seemed to have tactful ways of dealing with them.

Hatred stood up and said, "I'm sure you expect me to say something brilliant." He shrugged. "Well, I have an idea of what to do. As you all know that I can easily kill the people without much effort, I have various sophisticated means of dealing dangerously with the people. Once I take hold of the hearts of the people, you can be sure that they are going to break so many rules of their Lord. I cannot be easily noticed but when I strike, it is always a deadly blow."

"Good, good of you," Wickedness said.

Variance stood up and said, "it's my turn to share my idea, I suppose. Let me start by first saying that I am the least noticed but I destroy things easily. I can break the backbone of every organization. All I need to do before I strike deadly blow is to wait for the difference in the opinions of the people. Then I'll begin to remove the people's garments of Righteousness one by one. I will never allow the people to be in agreement because if there is agreement among the people, I'll not be able to operate. In fact, I

33

don't think anyone here would be able to operate successfully if there's agreement among people."

"You can speak for yourself!" Pride roared at him. "Everybody knows my operation cannot be deterred by agreement among the people."

"Nobody can hinder my operation too!'" Idolatry said.

Many other warriors began to boast about what they would do even if there was agreement among people.

"Silence!" Wickedness shouted angrily. "Why wasting precious time arguing over trivial things?" He paused to look at the warriors. "Many of you are not aware of many things though you're all great warriors. You're ignorant of one vital point, which Variance was trying to make. I think I better let you see that point. If the Conquerors are in agreement, we - all of us - are doomed! We'll be buried in one big grave without achieving a thing. In fact, the major strength of the redeemed people lies in agreement with one another. With that powerful armour of war, one will chase one thousand of us. And if two of them who are in agreement with each other use the same weapon, they will put ten thousand of us into flight."

All the warriors looked stunned.

Pride asked in shock, "you really mean just two redeemed people can be that powerful? What happens if more than two of them combine their efforts together to fight us?"

"That simply means a disaster to each one of us," Wickedness replied. "If we are able to get down any of the followers, he will stand up again with full force if the rest rally round him. There's no way we can deal with them if they are in agreement. You see, the basis of their agreement lies in the rules and standard which The Redeemer set for them. From the information I have at my disposal, their saviour has promised them that if they fall, they will rise again. If they are together, they will constantly remind one another of the rules. If any of them breaks the rules or lose his garment or if he is discouraged or he is wounded, others can easily revive him and bring him back to his feet. Often times, the revived warriors pose more threats to our kingdom. One of the wise sayings of The Redeemer is: 'iron sharpens iron; so a man sharpens the countenance of his friend.' That means that they need one another in the battle and in their struggles to get to Eternity. Once they appreciate this fact, we should expect outright defeat. I really don't know how we can survive it if the redeemed people come together as one.'

The warriors looked more frightened at the open confession. There was only one thing in their minds. If the redeemed people get to know the strengths in being in agreement with one another, the war is over even before it started.

Wickedness sensed their fright. He smiled and said, "you don't have to worry about that. It is part of the strategy to hide this fact from them."

"Supposing any of them get to know this, what is going to happen to us?" Strife asked.

"You think some of them don't know this?" Wickedness asked. "Believe me, they know.'

"What have we come here to do then?" Fear asked, terrified. 'We should be running for our dear lives by now because we really don't stand a chance to win this battle."

"And where do we run to?" Wickedness asked him.

"If we don't have anywhere to go, we can agree to become the slaves of redeemed people."

There was uproar of "NO!" among the warriors.

Wickedness gave him a long stare. If not that he needed him badly in the battle, he would have ordered him to be locked up in the dungeon or executed immediately. Besides, he could not afford to lose or discourage any of his warriors. Every warrior counts in the battle. While boosting their morale, however, he felt the need to be stern at the same time. He said in a deep voice, "if anyone gives in to any of our enemies or runs away from this battle, I'll personally cut off his head. So you either fight the Conquerors or you fight with me."

Fear bowed and said, "I'm sorry, our great king. You're the one that scared me stiff with the analysis of the strength of the Conquerors."

35

"You're supposed to scare them and not vice-visa," Wickedness said. 'I want all of you to get this straight into your heads. First of all, we have nowhere to run to. This is our kingdom. We must fight to defend it, no matter what is going to cost us. We've lost Eternity forever and The Father has decided to send us to Doom. I don't need to tell you how terrible Doom is. One of the reasons we have to go into battles with the people is because we want to have as many of them as possible to go down there with us. Besides that, the redeemed people can take over this kingdom from us before they eventually go to Eternity if we don't fight them. If that happens, that would be double tragedy. We'll become slaves before we are locked up in Doom. Can you stand that?"

The warriors roared, "No!"

Wickedness went on, "I can assure you that if each of you carries out his own part in the operation, there is no way they can come together. If Ignorance cannot destroy most of them, Variance or Strife or other warriors should be able to deal with so many of them. If one follower escapes from one warrior, he cannot escape from the other. Working as a team is crucial in this battle."

"That has not really answered the question of checking the power in the agreement among the redeemed people," Doubt said thoughtfully.

Wickedness smiled wearily. He could see that Doubt probably wanted to be convinced of his part. "It looks as if you overrate the power of the redeemed people and underrate our power, including yours. There is no one who cannot check that power. The people lack the experience which is crucial in the battle." He pointed at him. "Even you have what it takes to weaken that power with the use of weapons like scepticisms, distrust and suspicions. If you use those weapons very well, you can get us more victories than many other warriors." He looked at Doubt straight in the face. "Now talk to me warrior. Do you see your chances to check the power?"

"Yes!" Doubt said excitedly.

Wickedness looked at the rest and said, "like I said, if we work as a team, we have enough weapons and tactics to check the power. We can make up for the weakness of each other and improve on our strategies if we work together. I can think of some ways to improve our tactics as each of you shared your ideas. For instance, while Pride was telling us his plans, he probably did not realize that he can use weapons like ego and dignity to destroy the potential of some of the people that war against us. He has what it takes to prevent some of the people from accepting the fact that there is power in agreement from those who know about it. That attitude alone is enough to make any follower of The Redeemer to fall. The Redeemer warned the people by saying, 'Pride goeth before destruction, and a haughty spirit before a fall.' In essence, The Redeemer knows that Pride can pave ways for some warriors to destroy the people. If Pride can use a very strong rope like haughty spirit to tie the people, it would be impossible for them to see what is coming to hit them even if they are well informed by others. Besides that, Doubt can blindfold them with materials like stormy situation and impatience. That'll make them to lose confidence in the armour. Once they lose confidence in their weapons, it would be very easy to take them from them. Fear can easily use a weapon like panic or fright to chase them round to the place other warriors can easily deal a deathblow with them. We really cannot exhaust all our tactics and our potentials before we destroy most of the redeemed people. I don't want you to think that our enemies are smart. They are so stupid that The Redeemer once admitted before them that even our salves are wiser than them. Despite their weapons that are far more superior to ours, Ignorance alone is enough to destroy so many of them."

All the warriors were so excited that roared with joy again.

"Our greatest advantage," Wickedness continued, "is not in what we want to use to fight with them but it lies in their stupidity and lack of information or knowledge. They may have the power that can easily earn them victories but most of them don't even know it. Those who know it will not use and apply it because they don't know that it means everything to them. Other warriors would attack these who use it and follow the rules of The Redeemer. At the very least, we can avoid them and make them unpopular if they try to teach others. Ignorance will hide important truths from as many people as possible, most especially those who are not willing to learn from others. We have enough warriors that can deal with each of the people, including the slaves, according to their levels and understanding of the rules. So you don't have anything to worry about."

He waved at Variance to continue from where he stopped.

"As we have been made to understand now that agreement among the redeemed people can cause a disaster," Variance said, "my best shot is to bring a lot of differences among the people. I will cause them to be at loggerheads. I will not allow them to see any reason they should be in agreement. Through that, well strip them of the power in coming together as one."

"That's very beautiful," Wickedness said.

Emulations said, "I will cause the redeemed people to live according to the pattern of our slaves. With the use of weapons like materialism, latest fashion and other things, I will influence them to replace their garments with another material, which is commonly used by our slaves. I'll also let them feel pleasant and beautiful if they live and behave like our slaves. Besides, I will make them copy other people in everything they do. Once they begin to live the life of others, they will never be able to fight us with the armour of war."

"That's good," Wickedness said.

Wrath stood up and said, "you know I don't take nonsense from the redeemed people. I will use intolerance, provocation, complaint and weapons like that to remove their garments of Righteousness."

"Just like that?" Wickedness asked suddenly. "How would you do that?"

"Well, it's a simple trick really. I will plant intolerance among the redeemed people while provocation would be hanged around them like a time bomb. Intolerance will be used to cause little thing to happen. Provocation will drop and explode. Once it explodes, the people will put aside the armour and go after each other's necks. I will lead other warriors like Malice, Lack Of

Forgiveness, Accusation and others into their midst and disarm the people of the armour. Apart from that, I will personally tackle the mysterious soldier of Comforter called Love."

"You can handle that deadly soldier?" Wickedness asked excitedly.

"Of course, I can!"

"How? Talk to me, warrior."

"Well, it's a simple strategy really," Wrath said. "You know Love cannot stay where I'm operating, especially if I use provocation as a weapon. If Love stays where I'm operating, he either kills me or I kill him."

"You must not allow him to kill you, you fool!" Wickedness roared. "You must flee from him if you see that he wants to strike you. That soldier is simply deadly. I told you he can destroy so many of us at a go and bring back to life the enemies we have killed already."

Again the warriors looked stunned. Now they were beginning to wonder why they have to fight the redeemed people. If, after doing all they could to destroy them, they still come back life, what would be the essence of fighting and killing them? Perhaps Fear was right to think that surrender was the only option they have. After all, there is no point in killing the enemies that would still come back to life once Love intervened.

As usual, Wickedness sensed their concern. He smiled at them with assurance. "It's not that easy to bring back to life a dead follower of The Redeemer. In fact, before he knows that he's dead, he would be rotten in our territory. So there is nothing to really worry about in a dead follower of The Redeemer coming back to life. I just feel the need to let you know that Love is capable of restoring a dead follower if the Conquerors can give him the chance. The truth is: nobody would give him the chance." He looked at Wrath. "I don't want you to underrate the power of Love by getting close to him."

"I won't let him get at me at all. At least, I have a way of driving him away with provocation, intolerance and complaints."

"Now I want all of you to note this: if you see Comforter

around any follower of The Redeemer, make sure that you drive him away first before you attack the person," Wickedness said and looked at them round. "Do you all understand?"

They all needed.

"Comforter commands so many deadly and mysterious soldiers. If you don't drive him away, you will only get everyone of us here into big trouble," he added and waved at Wrath to continue after a while.

"I will influence some of the people to get mad at every little thing in their Congregations. They would be too angry at one another that they would not have time to face us in the battle. I will also cause them to be furious at their Captains each time they tell them the truth that can help them. With that kind of attitude, they will not be effective with the use of the armour of war."

"Good, good of you," Wickedness said.

Strife stood up, looking stern at the people. "You know I'm a trouble maker. I'm an expert in making trouble with proven record of success at Antioch, Syria and Cilicia. I can turn the whole battle against us into competitions and boosting of egos among the redeemed people. They would be so involved in this competition that they would not have time to fight us. Such competitions can make them lose focus in the real battle and breed conflicts among the people. And, of course, that can divide them. You've been talking about agreement. With my presence in the warring team, there is no way the redeemed people can stay together. Remember, once they are not together, they shall fall and die together!"

"Good, good of you!" Wickedness said.

Sedition stood up and said, "as we have been informed that the people must follow and apply the rules The Redeemer has given to them before they can be victorious, I will see to it that they don't follow the rules. All I will do to make them disobey the rules is to whisper something contrary to the words of The Redeemer into their hearts. Once they take what is different from what they had been told, they will not be effective with armour, especially the sword. Remember I have a record that proves that I can do it. Lust Of The Eyes referred to the case of First

Couple. If I had not helped him, he would probably have failed to make them eat the forbidden fruits. In the real sense of it, I helped Lust Of The Eyes to succeed. What I did them was to whisper into their ears, 'Can you see that it is very good to eat that fruit?' "

Lust Of The Eyes sprang on his feet in anger and said, "I did that all alone! You didn't help me!"

"'Now, now," Wickedness said impatiently, "there's no need to argue over that. What both of you should do is to team up and fight the redeemed people together instead of arguing. I don't want someone to come here, bluffing. I want results! I want the redeemed people dead! So we cannot afford to waste time bluffing or arguing."

Sedition and Lust Of The Eye looked at each other, smiled and then came together to form a team.

"Let me sound a warning here," Wickedness said. "Just as we can easily defeat the redeemed people if they are not in agreement, we can also be defeated if you are at each other's necks. You must work as a team, not in isolations. I don't want anyone of you coming here, claiming to be a hero. We are all heroes as long as we can get results. Do you understand me?"

"We do, oh King!" the warriors chorused.

Wickedness nodded at Heresies to share his ideas.

Heresies stood up, looked at Wickedness and said, "You know that I am a spy, my lord. I supply you the true and the distorted versions of words of The Redeemer. So I have to work alone."

"I understand your position," Wickedness said, "but you still have to work with others." He looked at the rest. "I insist that you all work together. That's a law. Anybody that breaks it will incur my wrath."

"Okay, my lord," Heresies said. He looked at the rest and continued, "I am simply a deadly warrior. I can create rooms for as many warriors as possible to invade the Congregations of the redeemed people and deal with them ruthlessly. I can do this by simply perverting the truth and twisting the words of The Redeemer. As you know that it is the words of The Redeemer that

41

set the people free, I can enslave them again with the perverted version of the words. I will use sex-before-marriage, a-little-alcohol-makes-no-difference-in-holy-living and other things like that to make the people directly or indirectly go against the rules that can earn them victories. I also have a way of destroying the garments of Righteousness with weapons like pervasion and distortion. Besides, I can bring up false Conquerors among our slaves and equip them with perversions and distortions. Once our enemies are having the perverted rules or standard, many warriors like Fornication, Drunkenness and many other warriors will have the chance to invade their Congregations and lead them to the place we can beak their scraggy necks."

Wickedness and the rest laughed, clapping. He said, "good, good of you, Heresies."

Envying stood up, feeling the need to impress all warriors. He said, "now I'm going to tell you what I have in stock for the people that are not successful with their endeavours. I will cause them to be envious of those who are successful. That will give Jealousy room to strike them. I will use weapon like hostilities to make them go against one another. Strive can come in and turn the battle into conflicts and competition among the Conquerors. Instead of fighting us, they will find themselves competing with one another."

"Good, good of you, Envying," Wickedness said. "I like that."

Murders stood up, looked round at his colleagues, feeling pleased with himself. "You know, of course, that I can disarm the redeemed people. All of you may think I'll carry a weapon before I kill the people. You are dead wrong if you think that's the way I'll operate. I'm a smart guy, you know. So I will disarm the people of their armour by using their mouths as weapons to kill one another."

"How will you do that?" Wickedness asked.

"I will need to work with Backbite before I can do that really," Murders said. "He would have to pave way for me with the use of weapons like rumours and false allegations against the redeemed people in other to discredit and kill them morally. Distrust and Hypocrisy will come to assist me as I put finishing touches to the plan. Before they know what has hit them, they will either be dead or serving us; thinking they are still redeemed people."

"Good, good of you, Murders," Wickedness said.

Drunkenness stood up clumsily. He looked a little sober that day. He knew better than to appear before the king in drunken stupor. Just like other warriors, he feared and respected Wickedness. He said, "you think I'm useless in this operation? I'm not. Once Heresies creates room for me in the Congregations as he promised, I'm as valuable as any of you. I can make them slumber and intoxicated by making them taste a little wine. Once they are intoxicated, I'll strip them of their garments of Righteousness and lead them to where other warriors will butcher them ruthlessly. You wouldn't expect them to fight us when they are intoxicated like this...." He staggered forward and backward as a form of demonstration.

The rest laughed as Wickedness said, "good, good of you, Drunkenness. You'll be more useful than I thought."

Revellings stood up and said excitedly, "hay, I cannot be dispensed with. I can disarm more people than any of you with my great tricks."

"I told you I don't want anyone bluffing here," Wickedness said.

"I'm not bluffing, my lord. I'm serious."

"Let's hear your idea if you are so smart."

"I can organize disco parties as I did in Sodom and Gomorrah. I'll take away the people's garments of Righteousness and give them the garments that are made with shame and disgust. I'll let Uncleanness to design all their cloths with filthy decorations in the name of Fashion." Revellings said, enjoying the interests and the attentions of others. He began to dance, talking as if he was singing excitedly. "Dig that! I can use weapons like entertainments and sophistications to divert the attentions of the people from The Redeemer and the promise of Eternity. As you

43

know that entertainment is a very powerful weapon to use against the people, we can use it to control their minds. I will create music that will strip the people of the entire armour and the presence of Comforter completely. Songs that are composed by our slaves who pretend to be the redeemed people will do the trick. Music like 'rock, rock and roll' will drive the people crazy! Dig that! They will rap, dance and sing like our slaves. The redeemed people will get carried away, especially if I introduce it into their Congregations. How do you feel if redeemed people dress shamelessly and dance in the Congregations to the tune of rock music or something crazy, thinking they are praising their Lord?"

"Boy," Wickedness said, looking excited and delighted. "You're really smart! Good, good of you."

He looked round at the warriors who were waiting for his next order. "Very soon, the redeemed people will begin to launch attack against us but since you have all ideas of how to deal with them, you don't need to worry about anything. By the time all of you are through with them, we would have captured many of them." He paused, nodding at them. "I'm glad I have clever warriors. Now you can go and work on your plans. Let me know all you need. You have all the slaves at your disposal. Equip them with all they need - money, beauty, head knowledge, talents - anything they need. Give them instructions of any kind through any means like entertainments and lectures. Speak any language they can understand. Use violence if you have to. They don't have to know that you're using them. If they know, they may not be very useful to you again. If you need anything from me, let me know immediately. We've got to work and fight the redeemed people. Fight them at every side, fight them left and right, fight them in their Congregations, fight them in the towns, fight them in their homes, fight them in the dream, in the Spirit, in the Mind, in the Flesh - anywhere, everywhere because we have but very short time. Use anybody - everybody that is available. Go, go, and get prepared, warriors."

"Yeaah!" The warriors shouted and then dispersed.

CHAPTER FOUR

The people just finished putting on the whole armour, which The Redeemer has given them. They gathered round him before they go into the battlefields to face Wickedness and his warriors.

The Redeemer looked thoughtful for a long time before he said, "I have so much to tell you but I cannot tell you now. Comforter will be with you everywhere you go. He'll teach all the things you need to know. Please, listen to him. You must obey everything he tells you because it is only through him I can have communion with you. As his name implies, he will comfort you when you are faced with difficult situation. Wickedness has designed so many ways to fight you. He has tactful warriors who are ready to fight you in battlefields called the Flesh, the Spirit and the Mind. The battle will be so severe that it will take only violent people to take Eternity by force. You must not walk in the Flesh, not to talk of fighting there. If you walk in the Flesh, the violent warriors of Wickedness like Adultery, Fornication, Uncleanness, Lasciviousness, Idolatry, Witchcraft, Hatred, Variance, Emulations, Wrath, Strife, Seditions, Heresies, Envyings, Murders, Drunkenness, Revellings and a host of others will launch deadly attacks against you. The weapons of your warfare are not to be used in the Flesh though they are mighty enough to pull down strongholds. You should therefore walk and fight in the Spirit. That's where you can be victorious. Comforter will give you

45

soldiers like Love, Grace, Joy, Peace, Longsuffering, Gentleness, Goodness, Faith, Meekness, Temperance and so many others that will help you fight the battle in the Spirit.

"Wickedness will also fight you in the Mind. You must push the battle to back to the Spirit with the sword and shield. Imagination is one of the warriors that are waiting to fight you in the Mind. He has terrible weapons like evil-thoughts, hurt-feelings, self-condemnations, indignations, accusation, wrong-impressions and misunderstanding which he had been using over the years. Doubt is another dangerous enemy warrior that is good at fighting in the Mind. Don't give him room in the Mind. If you do, he can disarm you of the armour and make you vulnerable to the attack of other warriors like Suspicions, Complaints, Inferiority Complex, Failures, Self-Pity, Faithlessness and Remorse. You need to fight him with the combination of the sword and shield if he attacks you all. Fear is a dreadful looking enemy who is not even as strong as he looks. Actually he is a toothless dog that roars and looks like a lion. The only thing he does is to create room for other warriors like Compromise, Backslidings, Destruction and others to attack you. He is not an attacker. He only takes away people's strengths by roaring as loud as he can. He is really good at frightening people with his roars. Once you let any of these warriors to engage you in the battle in the Mind instead of you to resist them, you may lose your strengths and vision.

"You must let Courage hang around you. Wickedness will make your faith in me look like insanity but if you keep to my words, you will be more than conquerors. If you keep your sanity in the kingdom that is full of insanity by living by the standard I gave to you, you shall behold my face in Eternity. A time will come when Wickedness will make this kingdom very inhabitable for you unless you compromise my standard and surrender to him. I tell you that anyone that conforms to the standard of this kingdom after you have been redeemed is like a dog that goes back to his vomit. Such person has no part in the Kingdom of my Father in Eternity. Sometimes, I can make use of some people who are saying but not doing what I said as borrowed vessels to deliver others from Bondage and the slavery of Wickedness but when it is time to take my people to Eternity, I will say to them; 'I know you not. Depart from me, you workers of iniquities.'

"There is something so vital you all need to do. You need to be in unity. There is power in unity. I therefore want you to be of one body. The body is not of only one member but many parts. If the foot shall say, 'because I am not the hand, I am not of the body; is it therefore not of the body?' If the whole body were an eye, where were the hearing? If the whole were hearing, where were the smelling? But now I set the members, every one of you in the body as it pleased me. And if you are all one member where were the body? But now are they many members, yet but one body. And the eye cannot say to the hand, 'I have no need of you,' nor again the head to the feet, 'I have no need of you.' No, much more those members of the body, which you think to be less honourable, upon these you bestow more abundant honour; and your uncomely parts have more abundant comeliness. For your comely parts have no need; but I have tempered the body together, having given more abundant honour to that part which lacked: That there should be no schism in the body, but that the members should have same care one for another. And weather one member suffer, all the members suffer with it; or one member be hournored, all the members rejoice with it." He paused for a long time. Tears began to drop from his eyes, "you are the ones that form my Body and members in particular. This Body of mine is called Congregation. I don't want you to shatter my body by getting divided."

The people too began to cry.

"I'm a man of sorrow," The Redeemer said. "I left my glory and kingdom in Eternity because of you. Please, I beg of you, do not allow Disunity to dwell among you. A time will come when Wickedness will send him to your midst. He is so dangerous that he can make you powerless. Nothing can defeat an enemy like that among all the weapons of war I have given you except one of the soldiers of Comforter called Love. Only Love can keep you united. Only Love can give you the power to defeat Disunity. Love will make you care for one another the way you care for yourselves. Only Love will make you go into the mud to get your brother and sister if he or she falls inside. Only Love will make you go through pain and much suffering for the sake of others. Only Love can prevent you from seeing the faults of others. Only Love can teach you to carry the burden of others. When you carry the burden of others, yours becomes light because others will carry it for you. Love is so powerful that he can make you do anything for others, including laying down your life for their benefits. In fact, it was Love that brought me down to this kingdom to redeem you. Love will never give room for provocation and intolerance. Love doesn't die but he can grow cold if he is not given a room to operate. Love would make you feel very uncomfortable when others are in pains and sorrow. If others die in the battlefield, Love can help you bring them back to life. It is through Love that people would know that you're truly my followers. If any of you is defeated in the Mind or in the Spirit or in the Flesh, Love will make you feel it as your defeat and your defeat as the defeat of others. If any of you overcome any of the enemies, Love will make you see the victory as yours and your victory is that of others. Love makes you responsible for the blood of others while I hold each of you accountable for whatever goes wrong with them. The issue is not the defeats or the deaths of others that make you accountable but what you do within your ability to prevent them. So Love makes you your brother's keeper. Love will constantly ask you troubling questions like: 'Do you stab others at the back when they count on you to help them?' 'Do you stretch out helping hands to lift up those who have fallen?' 'Do you block your ears when others cry in pains or sorrow?' 'Do you visit those who are in prison?' 'Do you give those who are hungry food?' 'Do you clothe those who had been stripped naked?' 'Do you minister to the needs of others?' If you do any of these things to others, you have done it to me. Even if you speak with the tongues of men and of subjects of Eternity, and have not Love, you have become as sounding brass, or a tinkling cymbal. And though you have the gift of prophecy, and understand all mysteries, and all knowledge; and though you have all faith, so that you could remove mountains, and have not Love, you are nothing. And though you bestow all your goods to feed the poor, and though you give your body to be burned, and have not Love, it profiteth you nothing. Love suffereth long, and is kind; Love envieth not; Love vaunteth not itself, is not puffed up, doth not behave itself unseemly, seeketh not his own, is not easily provoked, thinketh no evil; rejoiceth not in iniquity, but rejoiceth in the truth; beareth all things, believeth all things, hopeth all things, endureth all things. Love never faileth: but whether there be prophecies, they shall fail; whether there be tongues, they shall cease; whether there be knowledge, it shall vanish away.

"With the power of Love in your midst, you will always be in agreement. If Love is missing, you will always be in disagreements. If you are not in agreement, you can never be effective with the use of the armour. Apart from that, Comforter who uses Love all the time will be grieved if Love is missing among you. Needless to say, Love is his most powerful of all soldiers of Comforter. The moment Comforter is grieved, you are on your own. Once you are on your own, Wickedness will recapture you as his slave and make your life more miserable than before. Therefore, you must be united; exhorting one another because iron sharpens iron. You cannot get a wood to sharpen iron. Only you can encourage one another."

Again The Redeemer paused, looking up. "I'll like to tell you a beautiful story about a tower called Babel.

"There were once a group of people who found a plain in the land of Shinar. They all decided to live in the place together.

"One day, the people said to one another, 'Go to, let us make brick, and burn them thoroughly.' And they had brick for stone, and slime had they for mortar.

"And they said, 'Go to, let us build us a city and a tower whose top may reach Eternity, and let us make us a name, least we be scattered abroad upon the face of the whole earth.'

"Around this time, I was with my Father in Eternity. The distance between the plain of Shinar and Eternity is so much that it would take the people millions of years to accomplish their aim.

"My Father and I kept quiet, watching the people

performing what seems incredibly stupid.

"Now this people had great strengths which are found in unity. And they kept on building the tower of Babel. We waited for something to disorganize them. We wanted one of them to grudge against the other but nothing of such happened. They kept working like teams of termites that are building a hill.

"Then my Father said, 'Behold, the people is one, and they have all one language; and this they begin to do, and now nothing will stop them from doing what they have imagined to do.' And so we have to confound their language in other to stop them.

"What I'm saying in other words is that there is mighty power in unity. That is why I told you that if two people agree that I should do a thing, I have to do it. While one person is chasing one thousand, two people can put ten thousand to flight if they are united. Can you imagine the number of enemies you will chase if you all united?"

"We shall unite!" all the people shouted.

The Redeemer smiled at them, nodding. "Now," he said, "I've appointed Captains among you but all of you are to function in one area or the other. So I'll give you gifts, which you will need for the edification of my body. Remember that the gifts are not for trading and they are not for the people who have them. They are to be used to minister to me, to one another and to the people in Bondage. As you all know that the eye is to be watchful of any danger that might be coming to the body and other parts are for the purposes of doing the body some good, the gifts are meant to help my body. Don't be tempted by the enemies to trade with the gifts. The moment you start doing that, you're walking in the Flesh. Like I told you, if you walk or fight in the Flesh, you would lose outright. You must count on me to provide you with everything you need in this kingdom. Trust me to meet all your needs and don't lean on your understanding. If my Father in Eternity can make the lilies so beautiful and feed the birds in the air, how much more you who are so precious to him. You are walking in the Flesh if you look for what the slaves are looking for. There are so many irresistible warriors that will use pleasures, sex, money, materialism, anger, violence and other weapons to fight you in the Flesh. If you stay long in the Flesh, Wickedness will get the chance to steal you from me, kill you and eventually destroy you in Doom."

"Lord," one of the Captains called Pastor said. By the virtue of his position in the Congregation, he was appointed and equipped by The Redeemer to feed the people with his word. "How will you get us to Eternity if anyone of us dies in any of the places Wickedness and his warriors plan to fight us? I wouldn't like to think that everyone of us here would survive in the war."

The Redeemer smiled pleasantly at him. "You have just asked a very vital question," he said. "Although I don't plan to tell you this but, since you have asked, I'm obliged to answer you.

"Well, after the end of the big fight in the Flesh, the Spirit and the Mind; I will descend from Eternity with a shout with the voice of Captain of my warriors, and with the trumpet of my Father, and those who died as my true followers will rise first. Then those who are still armed with the armour and with Comforter with them shall be caught up together with host of my warriors in the cloud to meet me in the air, and so shall you ever be with me. Therefore comfort one another with these words even when the fight gets so fierce."

"Is it not possible for all of us to get to Eternity, Lord?" another leader called Evangelist asked. Though by the virtue of his position, he champions other people to go to all areas and convert the slaves in Bondage into the redeemed people, all the followers are actually mandated by the Lord to perform the duty which is regarded as the great commission.

The Redeemer said, "I have done all I can to ensure that everybody gets to Eternity. In fact, no one has any reason for failing to get there. As many as believe in me and do what I command you to do will go to Eternity. Verily, verily I say unto you, if a man keeps my saying, he shall never see Doom. Notwithstanding that, many will still fail to get to Eternity. The reason is that many will be persuaded and influenced by the slaves in Bondage and the warriors of Wickedness to remove their

51

armour. Once anyone conforms to the standard or persuasion of this kingdom, leaving aside my words, shall be enslaved again."

"Lord," another leader called Teacher said, "I heard people talking about another way to Eternity. Is there really another way?" He is specially gifted and mandated to teach and build the followers into Conquerors with the word of the Lord.

The Redeemer said to him, "I am the way, the truth and the life: no man cometh unto the Father but by me. He that enters not by the door is a thief and a robber. Wickedness has a warrior called Religions. He has the duty to make people feel that there are other ways to Eternity but the truth is: he is a destroyer that leads ignorant people to the lake, which burns with fire and brimstone. Other warriors that look like him are Customs, Works and Values. These warriors know how to persuade people to accept them as alternative ways to Eternity."

Again he smiled at the people and said, "I am the light of this kingdom. Whosoever believes in me would not dwell in Bondage. Whosoever desires to know the truth shall know. And whosoever shall know the truth shall be made free from Bondage."

Another leader called Prophet said, "Lord, for how long are we going to fight before you come to take us to Eternity?" He is gifted with the ability to foresee danger ahead and instruct the people of what needs to be done. He is also mandated to relate the mind of the Lord to the people.

The Redeemer said, putting his hand on his shoulder smilingly, "I do not know. Only my Father knows the time he has set to judge this kingdom."

"Could you tell us the signs of your second coming, Lord?" Apostle, another leader asked. By the virtue of his position, since he has direct contact with the Lord, he is mandated to move from one Congregation to another, strengthening the people with words of encouragements.

"The signs are in the sun and in the moon and in the stars: and upon the earth, distress of nations with perplexity: the sea and the waves roaring, men's hearts failing them for the power of Eternity shall be shaken."

52

Again he smiled at them, giving them assuring stare. "There are many things you don't know but you don't have to worry about that. When Comforter comes to you, he will tell you what to do." He looked round at the people. There are so many of them. "Are you now ready to go into battle with Wickedness?"

The people nodded and lifted up their weapons of war that are apparently invisible though they could be perceived in their conducts that they have the whole armour.

Then The Redeemer said, "be still and know that I am the Lord: I will be exalted among the heathen, I will be exalted in the town of Wickedness."

"Oh, yeeaah!" The people roared.

Then they began to sing, matching to the town of king Wickedness.

For this Lord is our Lord forever
And ever, he will be our guide
Even unto death!
Be still, says the Lord, and know
That I am the Lord!

CHAPTER FIVE

Wickedness and his solders have carefully studied all the words The Redeemer has given to his people. Heresies who has the mission of distorting or perverting everything The Redeemer has said in order to lead the people astray had gone to the Congregations of the redeemed people to spy. He noted that The Redeemer did not tell the people much except to give them the armour, teach them how to use it and promise to send them Comforter who would inform them all they need to know. He also observed that he counts so much on Comforter to teach the people everything and to give them insight into his words. It looks, however, as if the people are too ignorant to understand how important Comforter is to them in the battle.

What actually borders Wickedness apart from the armour of The Redeemer is the presence of Comforter in the life of his follower. He knew that with him around the people, nothing could be hidden from them. Comforter who knows all things would reveal to them all he had planned to use against the people. He could not quite comprehend the love of The Redeemer for the people. He loved them so much that he died for them. When he caused the people to hang and kill him on the tree like a criminal, he thought the mission to redeem the people from him was over. He did not know that he just drew the battle line. He did not expect him to love the people to the extent of not only leaving his throne in Eternity for the freedom of the people but also going to the extent of giving himself as a sacrifice for their redemption. This seemed absurd if not crazy. The Redeemer whom he knew as King of kings and the mighty God who created all things went to the extent of living with the people he created. He remembered how The Redeemer had come into the kingdom. Before the formation of the kingdom, The Redeemer was living inside the Father in Eternity just like a baby in the womb of his mother. When the Father wanted to create the kingdom, he sent The Redeemer who was then called 'The Word' out through his mouth. The Word came out of the Father to create all the things before returning back to him. He did this for six days after which 'The Word' rested inside the heart of the Father. Later he, Wickedness took the dominion of the kingdom through a cunning way from First Couple. First Couple were the ones given the power to posses the kingdom. The Father did not like the way he took over the kingdom and the way he used the people as slaves. But, apparently, there was nobody in Eternity the Father could send to the kingdom to redeem the people from Wickedness and his warriors. So, The Word who had been resting inside The Father since the creation was completed decided to come into the kingdom through a woman called Mary to redeem the people. Wickedness was happy when the people in the kingdom do not recognize The Word as The Redeemer. But his fear is that as many as receive him, to them the Father gives the power to become his children, even to them that believe on his name.

"Hmm…" Wickedness thought aloud with great concern. "Well, I don't have to border myself much about that." All his warriors have come up with good plans on how to destroy the redeemed people. His favourite warriors are Ignorance, Fear, Variance, Heresies and Complaints with his twin brother called Murmurings. They hardly made issues out of their achievements like other warriors even though their methods of operations are so subtle and deadly that only well-trained and seasoned Conquerors could detect and curb them. Ignorance is good at hiding information that is vital in making the people victorious. Since both the Conquerors and the slaves could be very dangerous to deal with if they are equipped with information, Ignorance makes them uninformed and therefore vulnerable. He makes it very easy for other warriors to destroy them.

Fear is good at threatening most of the Conquerors with darts like sickness, weakness, affliction, tribulation, distress, persecution, famine, nakedness, peril and sword. He is skilful in turning unreal weapon into real one. He is good at fighting in the Flesh, the Spirit and the Mind. He could easily make even well equipped followers to take to their heels in the battlefield through the use of illusion, circumstances and other weapons. He looks so deadly that Comforter ensures that one of his soldiers called Courage always stays around to drive him away from the people.

Variance is really an indispensable warrior. He is to ensure that the redeemed people do not form the kind of alliance that can easily give them victory.

Heresies is very good at distorting facts. Although he never boast of what he has done like many of the warriors but he actually aided the taking over of the dominion of the kingdom from First Couple by just adding a word to the information the Father had given them. He would never forget how it happened in the Garden of Eden. The Father warned First Couple, "of every tree of the garden, you may freely eat but of the tree of knowledge of good and evil you shall not eat for the day you eat of it you shall surely die." Heresies later went to the Woman and said, "you shall surely not die if you eat of the fruit of knowledge of good and evil." The word: "NOT" that was added to the warning was what persuaded First Couple to eat the forbidden fruit. That was what made it possible for him to take the dominion of the Kingdom from them. With the operations of Heresies in the warring team, the people who do not study the rules of The Redeemer but relying only on what their Captains tell them would be led astray. Since the people need the truth before they could be free indeed, Heresies has the duty to distort the truth and keep them perpetually in Bondage. Before they know they are far away from Eternity, they would have found themselves in Doom, the lake of fire and brimstone.

Complaints is simply good at breaking agreements and

relationships among the people. He has the skill to strain the relationship between the people and The Redeemer. His presence among the people alone is enough to drain their power. He is good at making the people be at loggerheads with Comforter. Once they are loggerheads with the person who is their main source of strengths, they are dead before they know it. He remembered how Complaints with his twin brother, Murmurings made the Father to destroy the people of Israelites when they were on their way to the Promised Land.

In spite of these deadly warriors whose skills could be relied on, Wickedness is still worried about Comforter and the armour. If the people are not so mindful of the whole armour and Comforter, he and his warriors stand a great chance to destroy the redeemed people once and for all without efforts. His concern is that many of the people may be mindful of them. Any follower, irrespective of his age or sex or training could easily wreck havoc into his kingdom if he is mindful of them. This reminds him of the story of a boy called David who was given physical armour. David knew all he needed was the armour of The Redeemer, which he used to defeat a giant warrior called Goliath.

And there was this other young man called Joseph who equally overcame one of his warriors called Adultery with the use of armour of The Redeemer. All his warriors gave beautiful testimonies of their present and past victories but none of them shared the testimonies of his total failures. There were many people in history that defeated him and the warriors outright. They even went as far as putting them into an open shame. Of course, he knew better than to remind them of their heroic failures. He needs them so much in the war that he could not afford to discourage them by reminding them that each of them had at one time or the other failed to carry out his mission. For this reason, he must not rely so much on them. Although the redeemed people may look ordinary and easy to defeat but their weapons of war are far more destructive than anyone can imagine it among them. The Redeemer had warned them not to fight his warriors in the Flesh. That is very vital information for he hopes to fight the people more in the Flesh than in any other places. Most of his warriors are good at fighting only in the Flesh. They stand little or no chance to overcome them in the Spirit for Comforter is always there to fight for them in the Spirit and even in the Mind. Besides, their weapons of war are much more effective only if they fight in the Spirit. He would never make the mistake of underrating them or engaging them in the battle in the Spirit. In fact, he is so scared of fighting them in the Spirit that the thought that The Redeemer has revealed this fact to the people makes him to panic secretly.

He looked up thoughtfully and heaved a sigh of concern. "I think I need to get more warriors," he thought. "Even then.... I still have to take part in the fight because we are not match for this person called Comforter. I must work day and night non-stop, working on strategies on how to steal, to kill and destroy the people before The Redeemer comes to take them to Eternity."

Wickedness sent message to another batch of warriors called Lovers Of Themselves, Lovers Of Money, Boasters, Blasphemers, Disobedient To Parents, Unthankful, Compromise, Unholy, Unloving, Unforgiving, Slanderers, Without Self Control, Brutal, Despisers Of Good, Traitors, Head Strong, Haughty, Lovers Of Pleasures, Form of Godliness But Denying Power of The Redeemer, Hypocrisy, Deceit, Unfaithfulness, Unbelief, Vanity and many others like that.

The warriors came and Wickedness had a brief meeting with them. "As you are aware that I have formally declared war against the redeemed people, I have invited you to team up with other warriors that are prepared to fight them. The Redeemer has given the people the power to deal ruthlessly with us. They have the power to take serpents without being harmed. If they drink or eat any deadly thing, it shall not hurt them. If they lay hands on those who are attacked with darts like sickness, they shall recover. These people are out to deliver our slaves from us. They have been given power to set free those we have kept in Bondage as slaves. I can never overemphasis the power of these people. However, they have one great weakness. Most of them do not know how powerful their weapon is. Ignorance has hidden a lot of vital information from most of them. So we have a lot of chances to defeat so many of them.

"First of all, Unbelief needs to ensure that other slaves do not believe at all in The Redeemer. Unfaithfulness must ensure that he creates circumstances that will make the people unfaithful in their dealings and make them lose their trust in the power The Redeemer has given them. Lover Of Pleasures must give them beautiful things, which they can enjoy in Bondage in exchange of their freedom. I don't have to tell you all I require from you. I trust your abilities but I want you to devote a lot of time on how to remove alliance among the people. We can achieve a lot in doing that. I'm counting on your abilities to do that.

"I want you to be mindful of an eternally powerful person with the people. He is called Comforter. He is a great source of concern to me. He has many mysterious soldiers who aid the people in fighting us. Without Comforter, the people are like herd of sheep, which we can butcher without expecting resistance from them. Comforter has a way of talking to the redeemed people. Once the people can hear and obey him, we are in serious problem that can cost us everything we've been controlling for a long time. I want you to make the people unconscious of him when he is talking to them. You must make them too stubborn, high-minded and proud to accept whatever he tells them. He is the main source of the power of the people yet he is the easiest being to push out of the life of any follower of The Redeemer. If we can succeed in pushing him out of the life of any follower, Emotion can replace him. With Emotion working in his life, there is no way he can know that Comforter is no longer with him. Being the most powerful and the greatest of all the gifts The Redeemer has given to the people, Comforter commands mysterious soldiers that are extremely catastrophic in our kingdom. The soldiers called Love, Grace, Joy, Peace, Longsuffering, Goodness, Faithfulness, Gentleness, Knowledge-Of-The-Word, Wisdom, Self-Control, Perseverance, Godliness and Kindness can render our attack against the redeemed people ineffective. In fact, each one of them is so destructive that we cannot afford to let anyone of them to fight alongside with our enemies. Love may look insignificant in this battle, but you must understand that he alone can destroy most of, if not all of the warriors. Not only that, he has the ability to restore and heal anybody that is wounded by the enemies."

All the warriors except Head Strong who looks stubborn were terrified.

"Well, Love is that powerful. In fact, it was Love that brought The Redeemer from Eternity. We really have to pay a serious attention to him. The first soldier you will notice in the life of any true follower of The Redeemer is Love. He is the most powerful soldier of Comforter. I can never over emphasis his strength among the redeemed people.

"The issue of Comforter is really a bad news for us. Our hope and target is to drive him away from among our enemies.

"Although no warrior, not even me can get close to any of the followers who stays with Comforter, but I have designed with other warriors ways we can remove or destroy the garment of Righteousness which the people would need before they can be effective with the use of the armour of war. The removal or destruction of the garment can make the people to grieve Comforter. Once Comforter is grieved, he would leave the follower of The Redeemer quietly. You can be sure that if he leaves the follower, he is as good as dead though he may think he is still alive.

"This war is not the battle of power because, as a matter of fact, their weapon is strong enough to pull down any of our strongholds. In the area of power, we are not match for the people. That is why we have to make it a battle of wisdom and strategies. Any follower can easily be defeated, no matter how great he is if he does not yield to the leading of Comforter. We have all the chances to win because many of the people love pleasures. Some are greedy and selfish enough to ask The Redeemer of the material things they tend to gain if they continue to fight. They never think of what they tend to gain in Eternity. Some are so blind that the weakest of our warriors can lead them to where they could be destroyed. We are going to deal with each follower according to his weakness. The type of warrior that would be assigned to a follower will be determined by his weakness. While Fear would be assigned to any timid follower, Unfaithfulness would make those who do not see beyond their noses to be unmindful of Eternity. If they don't know where they are going or when they will get there, they would give up the fight. Compromise has a lot of work to do. He must stay put with all the followers, looking for opportunities to open the door for other warriors to strike them dead.

"I must say, however, that there are some followers we must avoid. These followers are so violent that any attempt to get at them would be a suicide mission. They are fanatical soldiers of The Redeemer who are determined to crush us. If they are going about in our kingdom, please, don't try to stop them. They are too dangerous for us. Treat them like bunch of high explosive that can destroy our entire kingdom. Only Backbiting and Slanders can harass such people. Even then, they cannot hurt them much because; irrespective of the harassments they are faced; they will continue to grow stronger because Comforter is always around them. He always tells them so many hidden things about Eternity and about us. Well, sometimes, Backbiting may succeed in shifting their focus from the battle through the use of a weapon like rumours if he stays at the back of the followers. If he succeeds shifting their focus, he may allow Wrath to attack them. Slanders can weaken Conquerors through the use of a weapon like character assassinations. Falsehoods and Deceits can lure the people from the battle in the Spirit where they can get victory easily to the Flesh where they can be blindfolded with materialism. Vanity can disguise as Prosperity in the Spirit and lure them to the Flesh where they will lose touch with Comforter.

"Although some Conquerors may not be defeated through Slanders, Falsehood, Deceits and Vanity but they can be stumbling blocks to other followers in the battle. Some people who look up to others as role models can fall in the battle. So Slanders and Backbiting can pick on the character flaws of the Captains of the people and use that as stumbling blocks that can make other people fall into our hands. Besides, some slaves who may want to become followers can easily be obstructed from accepting The Redeemer as their Lord and Messiah. Once rumours and character assassinations are effectively used, the faith in The Redeemer, Comforter and even in the armour would be seen as means to cajole the people. So no matter what these slaves are told about The Redeemer, it would not have effect on them. Eternity will look like a mirage to them. Slanders' most important duty, therefore, is to look for the Captains of the redeemed people to fight through character assassinations and rumours. Sometimes when a leader falls, it is always easy to capture the people he is leading. Our warriors like Backbiting, Gossiping and Slanders would need to use our slaves and as many of the redeemed people that make themselves available to be used as tools to destroy other people. Once they are used, you can dump them. When they do this, they will achieve two good results. The people who are hurt by our warriors will develop hostility against the people that are used as tools without thinking that we are the ones that actually hurt them. The second result is that the people that are used as tools will continue to make themselves available to us. So, one of our strategies to weaken the redeemed people is through weapons like characters assassination, rumours and destructions of credibility of the Captains of the redeemed people.

"The other warrior we also need to count on is Fear. He can use members of his big and terrifying family like Fear Of Trouble, Fear Of Pain, Fear Of Poverty, Insecurity, Fear Of The Unknown, Fear Of Losing Respect, Fear Of Opinion Of Other People and Fear Of Possible Danger to weaken the hands of the Conquerors in the war. The people are easily moved by what they can see. So we can use what they can see to frighten them to surrender. We have a lot of weapons we can use in this area. Each of the weapons is designed according to the weaknesses of the people. We have weapons that can be effectively used in the Flesh, the Spirit and in the Mind. We are really prepared to fight the Conquerors everywhere. If we all fight without giving up, we will reduced the number of people going to Eternity and prevent our slaves from going there. I hope I have made myself clear enough."

"Yes, Oh King!" all he warriors shouted. "Long lives the king!" They added before they dispersed.

King Wickedness sat down again all alone after the warriors have gone. He was satisfied with the number of warriors he has got so far even though he wished he could get more. The redeemed people have got more than enough enemies to engage them at the moment. He did not doubt the fact that even if he could not capture all the people before their Lord comes to take them to Eternity, he would have captured a very good number of them. "Even then," he thought, "if the redeemed people don't get enough soldiers to fight, I might have to reinforce."

Nodding and smiling indulgently, he said, "Oh, phew! The redeemed people will get more than they ever bargained for!"

CHAPTER SIX

The cries of war against Wickedness and the proclamation of the city of Eternity fill the whole kingdom, attracting a lot of attention.

The redeemed people shout, "the Spirit of the Lord is upon us; because the Lord had anointed us to tell the good tidings unto the meek. He had sent us to bind the broken-hearted, to proclaim liberty to the captives, and the opening of the prison to them that are bound; To proclaim the acceptable year of the Lord, and the day of vengeance of our Lord; to comfort all that mourn, To console them that mourn, to give unto them beauty for ashes, the oil of joy for mourning, the garment of praise for the spirit of heaviness; that they might be called Trees of Righteousness, The planting of the Lord, that he might be glorified."

The people print tracts and distribute them to the people at various places in the kingdom. They hold meetings where Evangelist tells the people about The Redeemer. More and more people are converted to The Redeemer.

Pastors gather the new converts to Congregations and begin to give them the armour of The Redeemer. The converts also soon become Conquerors.

For a long time, the redeemed people seem to be getting victories. Every one of them is happy, especially when they see more and more people becoming the redeemed people.

Then the warriors of Wickedness begin to strike

unexpectedly as they grow in numbers.

Fear leads members of his huge and horrible looking family into the Congregations of the people. Fear Of Persecution, Fear Of Uncertainty, Insecurity, Fear Of Death, Fear Of People And Their opinions, Fear Of Daily Bread, Fear Of Losing Great Benefits and Fear Of Other things are among the soldiers that penetrate into the Congregations and attack the redeemed people. Many of the people take to their heels. Because the armour of The Redeemer is not covering their backs, their enemies are able to hit them at the back with fiery darts of Wickedness. They fall on their faces and die. The armies take their dead bodies to Wickedness who throws them into a bottomless pit. The armies of Fear never overcome many other people who know they could not win a battle by running. They fight like grants and get victories over their enemies. They remember what The Redeemer told them when he said, "behold, they shall surely gather together, but not by me. Whosoever shall gather together against thee shall fall for thy sake... No weapon that is formed against you shall prosper, and every tongue that shall rise against you in judgment you shall condemn... You shall tread down the wicked; for they shall be ashes under the soles of your feet."

By this time, the redeemed people have suffered much causality. A lot of followers have ended up in the bottomless pit while many are wounded and receiving treatment in the Congregations.

The redeemed people get themselves organized again after losing so many people to the enemies. Evangelists continue to organize and speak at meetings where many slaves are converted to The Redeemer. Pastors take them to the Congregations as usual and begin to give them the armour of The Redeemer. Teachers teach them how to use the amour and Prophets warn them of the danger in not using the weapon against warriors of Wickedness. Apostles get the people more organized, moving from one Congregation to another in order to ensure that none of them departs from the words of The Redeemer.

The warriors of Wickedness retreat for a while but they

soon strike again.

Pride sneaks into the Congregations and pretends to be part of the people. He manages to influence one of the Captains called Know It All and makes him feels and talks as if he knows everything. He thinks no one is capable of teaching him even though there was still a lot he does not know or understand.

Another leader called Captain Careful said, "Captain Know It All, you need to learn from others. You may be gifted in teaching but that does not make you the island of knowledge. So you still need to learn from others."

"If at all there is anyone to teach me, do you really consider a baby Captain like your type as my teacher? When did you know The Redeemer in the first place? I've been teaching people about The Redeemer long before you were born."

Captain Careful is a little hurt but, with the presence of Love around him, he is able to get over his hurt feeling quickly. He says gently, "I don't mean to cause any conflict between us. Remember what the Lord means when he said, 'Only by pride cometh contention but with the well advised is wisdom.'"

"So you mean to say I'm proud?" Captain Know It All says. "You might have to apologize for that."

"I'm sorry if you feel bad about that but what I actually mean is that we learn from one other," Captain Careful says. "It's a sign of humility if we are willing to learn from anyone who is saying things that in line with the word of the Lord, irrespective of the way he says it and irrespective of whom he is being an adult or a suckling child. The truth is all that is important to us."

"I'm yet to see the truth you want to share with me if you really have any to share."

Captain Careful sighs. He wishes he knows a more subtle way to point out the Pride that is trying to destroy him. He decides to use the words of The Redeemer again. "The word of the Lord says 'man's pride shall bring him down. But honour shall uphold the humble in spirit."

"Take a good look at you. You're quoting what you don't understand. What has pride got to do with what we are talking here?" Captain Know It All says in a patronizing manner with the intention to make him appear like a fool. "You don't even seem to have what it takes for anyone to listen to you. Besides, you talk like some one who never seems to have much knowledge."

Captain Careful looks offended but still, he feels the need to correct him with Love, knowing fully well that The Redeemer is unwilling to lose any of his people. He knows Captain Know It All is moving towards destruction. "Captain Know It All," he says gently, "I love you. That's why I have to tell you this. You see, humility is the ability to bend low even when you have every reason to feel so high. I think you are missing the point if you think anyone is too big or too smart to be corrected. Let me say this as an advice...."

"Keep your advice to yourself. I don't need it. If I'm to be advised, definitely, it is not by someone of your sort. You are too young and inexperienced for the position of my adviser."

Captain Careful is frustrated because Captain Know It All does not seem to see the enemy around the corner, trying to look for ways to destroy him. Captain Careful needs not to be told that he is under the influence of Pride that makes him not teachable and unwilling to take corrections. He is very concerned about the people he is leading. With what The Redeemer has said in his words, he knows that sooner or latter, he is going to perish. He may even lead others into the same destruction. The word of the Lord says, 'the person who hardened his neck when he is rebuked shall suddenly perish without remedy.'

"Now listen for your own good!" Captain Careful tells him sternly. "I'm not the sort of timid Conquerors you think. I only care for your soul but if you have chosen to go through the part of destruction, I can't stop you. The word of The Redeemer says, 'the high way of upright is to depart from evil…. Pride goes before destruction and a haughty spirit before a fall."

Having been tightly gripped by Pride, Wrath struck Captain Know It All in the face. He clamoured on top of his voice, "you hit me with your tongue like that?"

"I didn't hit you. I only told you the truth."

"You're really rude to me."

"I better be rude to you than to let Pride destroy you."

"You just use your tongue to do what the words of The Redeemer warn us against. He said, 'and the tongue is a fire, a world of iniquity: so is the tongue among our members, that it defileth the whole body, and setteth on fire the course of nature; and it is set on fire of hell."

Realizing that the inability to stand by what he says is a sheer sign of weakness or cowardice or a form of character flaw, Captain Careful says, "I have not used my tongue wrongly. I only tried to correct you but you feel too great to be corrected. Unfortunately or fortunately, nobody is too great to be corrected if he's wrong."

"Okay!" Captain Know It All said, "We call it a quit from here. Don't you ever cross my path. If you do, you will be sorry."

Captain Careful at once sensed it that more enemies of Wickedness have teamed up with Pride. He could feel the presence of Malice and Variance trying to tie Captain Know It All with a rope that is made with discord. So he feels the need to use two of the soldiers of Comforter called Patience and Gentleness to set him free from them. He smiles and says gently, "my brother, the situation is not as bad as that."

But then, Pride has tied Captain Know It All so tightly that he could not be free. He clamoured, "who is your brother? I'm old enough to be your father! You don't expect me to accept stupidity as humility from a wiper-snapper like you." He briskly strides out, walking tall with some people. He goes on to found a Congregation.

The warriors of Wickedness feel so happy that they celebrate the victory that day. With the foundation of such Congregation that is influenced by Pride, they know the people would find it hard if not impossible to defeat them in the battle.

Most of the people in the Congregation of Captain Know-It-All do not have much of the word of The Redeemer in their hearts. Wickedness sends them a warrior called Head Knowledge to influence them in the teaching of word of The Redeemer. He makes them very unmindful of Eternity and teaches them only how to prosper in the kingdom. The people are taught only how they could make themselves comfortable in the kingdom rather than to do what The Redeemer has sent them to do. He makes it impossible for them to recognize some of the warriors that were attacking them. The people become so weak that it is a lot easy for warriors like Adultery, Fornication, Strife, Pride, Hatred, Variance, Backbiting and a host of others to move freely in the Congregation of Captain Know It All. The Congregation is so shattered that the people begin to dine with their enemies without even knowing it. Many of the Captains come into terms with their enemies, making friends with deadly warriors like Witchcraft, Drunkenness, Uncleanness, Fear and Emulations. Wickedness does not even border himself about them except when he wants to use them. He concentrates his armies on the Congregations that are waxing stronger and posing serious threat to his kingdom everyday. The Captains of such Congregations ensure that everybody follows the word of The Redeemer, converting many slaves in the kingdom to become followers, fighting the enemies and guarding themselves with the whole armour of The Redeemer. They even teach them songs like:

> *Even though Poverty hit me like hammer,*
> *I will never give room for Compromise*
> *Even though the enemies fight with me,*
> *I will never give up the fight*
> *No matter what comes my way,*
> *I will fight on till I see my Lord*
> *I have Comforter by my side*
> *I have the armour with me*
> *I have no reason to lose the battle*
> *So I will fight till he comes to take me...*

There are other Congregations, however, that are getting destroyed everyday. Enemies like Persecutions, Prayerlessness, Fear and his big family dealt heavy blow against them but

Conquerors like Apostles, Evangelists and Prophets quickly go to rescue those Congregations. They begin to revive the people, including those who are dying or already dead. With the support of these Conquerors, many of such Congregations are restored. They begin to get so powerful that the enemies have to retreat from them for a while. Others who are too weak and inexperienced to understand how much they need other redeemed people to help them deal with the armies of Wickedness continue to manage on their own. The fight, however, becomes so fierce for them to handle that many are forced to surrender part of their weapons like the shield and the sword, making them vulnerable to the darts of the enemies. Without the whole vital armour, it is easy for the enemies to make them grieve Comforter. Some, who manage to hold Comforter even though some of their conducts are contrary to the words of The Redeemer, appear as if they still are still powerful like the strong ones. The truth is that, according to what The Redeemer told them, they often times use his power to defeat some enemies but when he comes to take his people; he would say, "depart from me. I know you not, you workers of iniquities." He would only use such people as borrowed vessels to minister to others.

Through Faithfulness, Knowledge Of The Word, Wisdom, Grace, Love and Courage, so many redeemed people are able to convert more people. Before long, the warriors of Wickedness begin to have so much people to contend with in the kingdom. The battle is becoming too fierce for him and his warriors in the Spirit. So he takes the battle to the Flesh where people's homes are built, using their spouses or children or other relations to fight the Conquerors. He manipulates circumstances and turn situations against them. He gets so much victory through this way that he is encouraged to use the method to attack the people continuously. Even some of those who are not defeated through that are made to lose focus. They find cause to question Comforter why The Redeemer allows the battle get to their homes.

Wickedness also designs a way of causing frictions among the people through Variance, Strife and Holier Than Thou

Attitudes in all the Congregations as they grow. The warriors make some of the people to feel they are greater or better than others. There are warriors who disguise like Great Talents who are assigned by Wickedness to influence gifted followers with the intension to lead the people astray. Many of such gifted people are claiming to be better than the other. Consequently, there is more focus on the gifts rather than Comforter who gives them the gifts. Before they know it, the armour had begun to slip out of the reach of such redeemed people. The warriors of Wickedness are striking them at every side. They never relent in their efforts in striking each and every follower of The Redeemer. With the use of weapons like negligence or indifference, deadly enemies like Ignorance, Deceit, Falsehood, Vanity and many others warriors burst into many Congregations and take so many people captives. The presence of such powerful warriors invariably makes so many redeemed people weak. Instead of the Captains to be teaching the people the word of The Redeemer, they are busy constructing cathedrals. Rather than raising vibrant Congregations of people that will terrorize the enemies and convert slaves into the redeemed people, the Captains are busy executing projects that have no relevance to Eternity. Some even take advantages of the followers by asking them to give what they cannot afford. Some use the name of The Redeemer for commercial purposes, some use it for self-glory and some use it to boost their egos. Vanity is really having a good time diverting the resources of the followers into useless or unholy endeavours and competitions.

So many redeemed people and those who wish to become part of them become so discouraged and frustrated that they go back to Bondage where Wickedness has promised to make life comfortable for them. All the Congregations are feeling the heavy and brutal attack from the warriors of Wickedness who seem very determined to crush all of the people before the war is over. Wickedness has dug a big grave where he plans to give the redeemed people a mass burial. Many of the Congregations begin to feel that they are at the mercy of Wickedness. Some of the Captains come into terms with Wickedness who promises to leave them alone if they and their people surrender their armours. They agree and maneuver some members of their Congregations to put down their armours. In other to maintain the power, which they have surrendered to Wickedness, the Captains in some of the Congregations invited warriors like Religions, Enchantments, Witchcraft; Sorcery; Idolatry and Hypnotism to deceive and convince the people that the power of The Redeemer is still very much with them. The presence of these enemies influences the people to practice magic or witchcraft in the name of The Redeemer. Thinking that they are using the power of Comforter, the slaves in Bondage join the people in mass, causing the Congregations to grow rapidly. Without knowing it, the people are already serving Wickedness although they look as if they are actually Conquerors. All their activities, as genuine as they seem, do not bother Wickedness at all. They can claim to be the redeemed people if they like as long as he knows that they belong to him. They do exactly what redeemed people do. They even organize meetings and crusades. They request Captains who are under the influence and control of deadly armies like Heresies, Lies, Hypocrisies, Oratory and Deceit to speak to the people. In fact, the real redeemed people would have been easily deceived by their activities if Comforter does not tell them who they are.

CHAPTER SEVEN

Now that Wickedness has succeeded in getting some of the people back to him in the battle, he concentrates his military strengths on the powerful redeemed people who are fighting and ready to conquer. The remaining people who prove to be real Conquerors are really giving him nightmares every minute. So much of his secrets had been leaked to them through the help of Comforter. Comforter's mysterious soldiers are making the battle a terrible experience for him. Only two or three Conquerors would enter his territory and chase away several thousands of his warriors, making the slaves in the area his deadly enemies. To check this excesses, he sends out powerful warriors like Lust Of The Eyes, Desire For Riches, Desire To Build mansion, Desire To Be Gorgeous, Desire To Have The Best In Life, Desire To Be Fashionable, Desire To Be Sophisticated and Desire To Possess Many Things to invade all the Congregations that are ready to die for The Redeemer. What makes them very deadly is that it is extremely difficult to recognize these warriors as enemies. They all appear so mild, good and nice that before long they have influenced a great number of the redeemed people, including strong ones. Many of the Captains borrow a lot of their ideas, which invariably influence most of what they teach the people. The Captains teach the people how their lives could be comfortable in the battlefield rather than to make them more concerned about Eternity.

Comforter moves Captain Strong to react to what is happening in the Congregations. He said to the people one day, "the battlefield is not a place to feel comfortable! We brought nothing into this kingdom and it is certain that we shall take nothing to Eternity. And having food and raiment, let us be content. But they that will be rich fell into temptation and a snare, and into many foolish and hurtful lusts, which drawn men into destruction and perdition. For the love of money is the root of all evils; which while some coveted after, they have erred from the faith, and pierced themselves through with many sorrows. But thou, O redeemed people, flee these things. And follow after Righteousness, Godliness, Faith, Love, Patience, and Meekness. Fight the good fight of faith, lay hold on Eternity...."

He looks round at the people, most of whom do not like what he is saying. "I'm sure you know that these are not my words. They are the words of our Lord. If you seek what others are seeking after, you will miss the way. Let's take the whole armour of The Redeemer and let us continue to fight as if our lives depend on it. Really our lives and that of others depend on it. The Redeemer told us we should take his yoke because it is light. The armour he has given us is the yoke. You can't feel comfortable with that yoke because it is meant to fight, not to sleep. You either take the yoke of The Redeemer or the yoke of Wickedness who has sent his armies into our midst to destroy those who are ignorant or disobedient to the word of our master and Lord."

Because a lot of the people are under the influence of the armies of Wickedness like Variance, Lovers Of Themselves, Without Self Control, Disobedient To Parents, Unthankful, Lovers Of Money, Haughty, Lovers Of Pleasures, Head Strong, Despisers Of Good, Compromise, Form of Godliness But Denying Power of The Redeemer, Hypocrisy, Deception, Unfaithfulness and Unbelief; many of them react violently against what Captain Strong says. They call him names and begin to persecute him. He is not surprised at all. The Redeemer already said it that a time would come when the people would not tolerate sound doctrine. They will depart from faith and give heed to their enemies and counsel of Wickedness.

Since many of the Captains in Congregations are not willing to accept the words of The Redeemer any more, Captain Strong is forced to stay only with those who were willing to accept and die for the truth.

Again, Comforter moves a man called Brethren in one Congregation to warn the people. "Labour not to be rich! Set your mind on Eternity not on the things in the battlefield. This place is not our home! Let us not look at things that are seen but at things that are not seen. For the things that are seen are temporal but the things that are not seen are eternal. Although we may be troubled on every side, we cannot be distressed; we may be perplexed, but not in despair; persecuted, but not forsaken, cast down, but not destroyed. We must be careful not to take the baits of the enemies through the riches that are not given to us by The Redeemer. The Redeemer had given us all we need in the battlefield without having to look for what people in Bondage are looking for. The Redeemer even told us that we must be content since we have food and raiment. We do not need riches to fight in the war. All we need is Comforter and the whole amour of The Redeemer!"

The people almost stone him to death. "You've gone crazy! How can you say we don't need riches in the battlefield? Have you forgotten what the word of The Redeemer says? It says the riches of the enemies belong to us."

"Is that why you have to pursue riches at the expense of Eternity and freedom?" Brethren questions them. "You see, all the promises in the word of The Redeemer are general. They are not necessarily specific to each and every one of us. While that promise may be applicable to some people, the word which also says, 'ye lust, and have not: ye kill, and desire to have, and cannot obtain: ye fight and war, yet ye have not because ye ask not. Ye ask and receive not, because you ask amiss, that ye may consume it upon your lusts' may also be addressed to people like you. Go to now, ye, rich men, weep and howl for your miseries that shall come upon you. Your riches are corrupted and your garments are moth-eaten. But I, Brethren will be patient into the coming of The

75

Redeemer. I will fight with the armour of The Redeemer and with my last breath."

The people pick Brethren like a piece of broom and throw him inside a place called Wilderness.

Brethren finds himself all alone in Wilderness that is infested with snakes, thorns, scorpions and even violent armies of Wickedness all because he is doing what The Redeemer commanded him to do. Although he seems alone, he is having the whole armour of The Redeemer with Comforter and his mysterious soldiers who give him victories upon victories in the war, which ordinarily ought to have claimed his life. He fights with all the enemies and overcomes all the hindrances on his way as if he had a whole battalion of warriors behind him. Really, there are much more mysterious soldiers with him than he can perceive. A follower with the armour of war and Comforter is more than all the multitudes of enemies within and without. Grace strengthens him despite what he is going through. He gives unusual strength to any soldier of The Redeemer that is ready to fight to the finish.

The enemies try to cross his paths. He had to fight the armies of Wickedness with so much rigour. They are so much that he could not be too careful. Before long, all the warriors of Wickedness begin to dread him so much that they start shrinking from him. He crushes them with his feet shod as if they are mere ants. He steps over hindrances as if they are bridges for him to pass into victories. Everything gives way as he tries to fight his way out of Wilderness. Seeing that he is causing so much havoc, the warriors called Weariness and Discouragement are immediately dispatched to check his power. The warriors use a weapon called self-persecution to let him see what he would have gained if he had compromised like some other redeemed people. Self-persecution works on him so perfectly that before long, he gets fed up with the battle. He starts looking for where to rest. Alternatively, he wants Eternal Rest to take him to The Redeemer. He wants to report to him the activities of his people that are no longer following his word in the battlefield.

He finds a place called Comfort Zone to rest. The place is

directly opposite the narrow way. He put down his sword and shield. He lies down on the soft grass that grows by the high way, feeling dejected and thinking of what he had lost in the battlefields. He knows he is not supposed to be at the Comfort Zone, let alone to think of what he has sacrificed for The Redeemer. He is supposed to walk through the narrow way, the road to the Conquerors' Gate that leads to Eternity where The Redeemer is interceding before the Father to spare his people who are going to Doom every minute.

Comforter tells him one of his warriors called Promise to deliver the message of hope, which The Redeemer has written and sent to him from Eternity. Actually The Redeemer knows what he and other faithful followers are going through in the battlefield but Brethren seems too dejected and preoccupied to hear Promise clearly as he reads the message to him. The message is meant to remind him of Eternity and to motivate him to stand up again.

Reading from the words of The Redeemer, Promise says, "…For your sakes, no doubt, this is written: that he that ploweth should plow in hope; and that he that thresheth in hope should be partaker of his hope… Knowing, that as ye are partakers of the sufferings, so shall ye be also of the consolation…. That by two immutable things, in which it was impossible for The Father to lie, we might have a strong consolation… Blessed be the Father, which according to his abundant mercy hath begotten us again unto a lively hope… To an inheritance incorruptible, and undefiled, and that fadeth not away, reserved in Eternity for you… Behold, what manner of love the Father hath bestowed upon you, that you should be called the sons of the Father: therefore the kingdom of Bondage knoweth you not, because it knew me not… Beloved, now are you the son of The Father, and it doth not yet appear what you shall be: but you know that, when I shall appear, you shall be like me; for you shall see me as I am… And every follower that hath this hope in me purifieth himself…"

Brethren looks as if he is familiar with the words. He smiles wearily at Promise and says, "I have no idea how long I have waited for the coming of The Redeemer. So it's pretty hard to hang on now. As you can see, I'm all alone. Everything I have is denied of me. What else do I have to give?" He sighs. "If the Lord really cares for me, let him send Eternal Rest to come and take me to Eternity. It'll be a great favour, don't you think so?"

"I don't think so, Brethren," Promise says. "The vision to save those in Bondage and to minister to the redeemed people who are wounded is enough reason to get on your feet and fight on. If you go to Eternity and meet The Redeemer now while so many are dying in the battlefield, what would be your reason for going home so soon? If he shows you the parts of his body that were brutalized while saving you from Wickedness, what is going to prove that you also suffered while trying to seek freedom for others? Eternity is not all about an individual. It is about everybody in this kingdom. You know that the Father does not desire the death of anybody but that everybody will get to Eternity. Eternity is a joyful and beautiful place. Doom is a terrible place to go. If you know how terrible Doom is, you will do everything you can to prevent people from going there." He then reminds him of all The Redeemer has told him. He urges him again to get up and continue with the fight. "Brethren," he tells him, "this is not the time to rest. The time to rest will still come."

"How can I stand it?" Brethren suddenly bursts out into hysterical sobs. "Many of my friends have ended up in the bottomless pit. I told the people the truth, they almost stoned me to death. I've been through so much that I wonder if The Redeemer loves me at all."

"Believe me, The Redeemer loves you," Promise says. "He's always thinking of you in Eternity. He's groaning with pain because of the things that are happening in the battlefield. For every drop of tears you shed, he shed his blood because he loves you. Please, don't hurt him and yourself by thinking he does not love you."

"Then why does he delay in coming?" Brethren asks.

"The truth is: he wants everybody in Bondage to be afforded the opportunity to turn to him. Like I said, he loves everybody so much that he doesn't desire anyone to perish."

"But many of his people are dying and going to bottomless pit every moment of everyday!"

"Brethren, listen to me," Promise says gently. "You can't blame The Redeemer for anything. He has given his people all they need to overcome all the enemies and problems in the battlefield. But the truth is: a lot of people are going after the wrong things. The enemies are making them ambitious. You see, the battle in the Flesh is what most of the people have not learned how to fight. Fighting in this area is difficult for most people. That's the reason The Redeemer does not encourage walking in the Flesh. The place does not make them to know and to do the will of The Redeemer. Unless the place is deadened with the continuous use of the sword and protected with breastplate, they cannot withstand the pressure of the battle in the Flesh. Furthermore, they must be dead to their own will and be active to the will of The Redeemer. I'm sure you understand what The Redeemer meant when he said, "to be mindful of the Flesh is death."

Brethren is encouraged a little but he wants an explanation why he had to be battered just because he is trying to do the will of The Redeemer. Surely, he is not expected to think of the joy that awaits him in Eternity when he has loads of problem to tackle. Surely, he is not expected to jump up with joy with so much darts of the enemies like poverty, sickness and even deaths flying around among the people. He is not expected to hang on to the sword after spending long days battling with the enemies that keep coming from all sides as if they are immortal.

As if reading his mind, Promise began to sing.

Somehow, we will understand
When we get to the place of joy
Pains today will surely end
Sorrow today will fade away
When we get to Eternity
Keep on fighting, thou soldier
Precious souls are dying
While you nurse your wounds

79

Enemies attack the weak
As you rest in the battlefield
This is not a place to rest
Nor the time to wonder about
This is a time to fight to finish
A time to share hope with others
A time to tell of the joy in Eternity
A time to deliver the oppressed
And a time to save the dying people.

Still Brethren is not moved. He does not even know what to do with Promise who keeps urging him to arise and fight in the grossly fierce war against Wickedness and then expects great reward from The Redeemer. There is nothing really hopes for in the Comfort Zone except Eternal Rest. He decides to stay in the place until he comes. He is simply fed up with the life in the kingdom. He wants to stay put where he is or go to Eternity to rest just as The Redeemer has promised. That is all that counts to him at the moment.

CHAPTER EIGHT

Comforter is not comfortable with Brethren who seems determined to stay in the Comfort Zone. He again sends two of his soldiers to him. One of them is called Patience and the other is called Obedience.

Obedience looks at Brethren sternly in the face and demands, "what are you doing in the Comfort Zone? What do you think all The Redeemer has given you are meant for? Pleasure? Comfort? You're saved to serve. The Redeemer invested so much of his time training you. You have to justify those investments by fighting and helping others. The Redeemer sets you free. So you must seek to set other people free. He gives you Courage so that you can encourage others. He gives you Blessings so that you can bless others. He gives you gifts, not to let them lay dormant but to be used to edify his body. He gives you strengths so that you can strengthen others. He gives you Love so that you can love others. He cares for you so that you can care for others. He talks to you so that you can talk to others. He sacrifices himself for you so that you too can make sacrifices for others. Everything he gives you and does to you is not meant for you alone but also for others. If you don't give to the people what he has given you, they will pay dearly for it with the life in Eternity. Do you want that? Life is not all about you but about The Redeemer, his people, the people in Bondage before it comes to you. If you've lost the vision to reach out to others, which the Lord gives you, you have lost the vision

81

about Eternity. The word of The Redeemer says, 'where there is no vision, the people perish: but he that keepeth the law, happy is he. A servant will not be corrected by words: for though he understands he will not answer.' So many helpless people are out there, dying in the battlefield. You lie down there, trying to find an excuse for resting. How could you possibly feel so comfortable in a place of death? Tell me where is the vision to save those who are dying in Bondage. Where is the vision to help your brothers and sisters that are wounded in the battlefield? Let me tell what you don't know. As you stay here in the Comfort Zone, someone is paying dearly for it with his life in Eternity. How do you feel about someone who is supposed to help you in Bondage staying and having a good time in the Comfort Zone? Happy? How do you feel about someone who trades with other people's chances of redemption with comfort? Happy? I tell you: that's what you're doing, Brethren!"

Brethren marveled at him. He makes very valid points though he does not seem to understand his condition. What else is he supposed to do after all he has already done? There is silence as he continues to look at Obedience in the face. He is a tough and impatient looking soldier of Comforter. He holds a book called The Scriptures in his hand. He constantly looks through the book as if that is all that matters to him. It is obvious that he would not indulge him in anything that is contrary to what is in the book. "You can't blame me for anything," he tells him. "I did my best."

"Your best is bad enough," Obedience snaps, looking straight into his eyes. "Your best efforts could not rescue you from Wickedness. How can you possibly expect it to rescue others? Your strength is not needed here. The reason lies in the word of The Redeemer who said, 'He will keep the feet of his soldiers, and the wicked shall be silent in darkness; for by strength shall no man prevail.'"

"What else am I supposed to do now? I was actually instructed by Comforter to share the truth with the people but they persecute me. They almost stoned me."

"If you are as ignorant as the people, you will behave the

82

same way. Besides, you don't consider the reaction of the people when delivering the message. You consider the Lord who instructs you. Commander Comforter sends his soldiers like Promise and Love to you so that you can tolerate the people but you care so much about your wounds that you don't care to listen to them. You're so occupied with your problems that you don't see other people's problems. Get this straight, Conqueror: The Battle Of The Conquerors is not about you or how you feel or what you do but strict compliance to the command of your Commanding Office and your Lord. You therefore have no reason whatsoever to stay here. If you don't get out of here, I'll have to personally invite one of the warriors of Wickedness to deal with you."

There is a long silence. Patience knows Obedience is hard on him. That is his usual way of dealing with Conquerors who are expected to know better than to take the matter of Eternity with levity. He is so tough that he sometimes uses storms and warriors of Wickedness get Conquerors to obey the commandments of The Redeemer.

Brethren is sober. When he notices that he regrets neglecting his duties as a Conqueror, Patience says in a very gentle voice, "sometimes it's really hard to speak the truth to those who are under the influence of warriors of Wickedness. But still you have to tell them so that the Lord will not require their blood from you if they die in the battlefield. Before you can stand for the truth in the face of fierce Persecutions, you need our company. We have to be with you if you want to get to Eternity with others. Since it is essential that you follow all The Redeemer has commanded all his followers before you can be victorious, we'll assist you in obeying the rules." He points at Obedience who is glancing through the book. "You're to follow every instruction he reads to you in the book even if it is so difficult or inconvenient for you to carry out. My duty is to calm and give you assurance of the love of The Redeemer for you. Grace and Joy will continue to give you the strength to fight on in the battlefield even when the going gets so tough."

Obedience looks through the Scriptures before he stares at

him with stern expressions on his face. "You have violated a lot of rules in this law book of The Redeemer but he has not sent us to condemn or to judge anyone. He wants us to correct you with the word instead. The first rule, which you must follow, is to mediate and follow the word in this book day and night. Failure to do that will give Ignorance the chance to take the sword from you. Once your sword is taken from you, you may end up in Doom. That is one major problem which most followers, especially the new converts normally face." He looks at the book again. "Secondly, according to the book, you're not supposed to be here."

Going by the tone of his voice, Brethren knows at once that Obedience must be a very difficult soldier of Comforter to deal with though he knows he needs him.

"According to what I have here," Obedience continues in his usual stern voice, glancing through the pages of the book, "you're to redeem the time because the days are evil. Obviously, one of the reasons you cannot afford to waste time on anything is because more people are losing their lives while you tarry; doing nothing." Then he looks up at him and says with a smile that gives Brethren a relief. "I can understand your pain and frustrations in dealing with the redeemed people. Most of them have violated these rules. That's why it is difficult to deal with them. I can assure you that with Patience and me by your side, you can educate many of them.

"The golden rules which you have to teach the people are: to keep the unity of faith with other followers and allow Love to dwell among you; come what may."

"Lastly, you must not grieve Comforter with wrong attitude or by giving room for any warriors of Wickedness like Lovers Of Themselves, Pride, Whoremonger, Without Self Control, Disobedience To The Word, Unthankful, Lovers Of Money, Haughty, Lovers Of Pleasures and Head Strong to influence you."

He pauses for a while, looking steadily at Brethren. "Well, I suppose you have had enough from me for now. Get on your feet and get back to work now."

Brethren hesitates, thinking of how to get started.

Reading his mind, Patience said, "you need to start from where you are. A thousand mile journey begins with a decision and a concrete step."

There is silence.

Obedience looks impatient. He is obviously not the kind of soldier that would tolerate any follower who entertains Complaints or Procrastination. He is particular about strict adherence to the rules of The Redeemer because a lot of things depend on it.

He moves closer to Brethren, looks at his face as if trying to find out the best way to make him follow his command. He pulls him up on his feet and shakes him violently, shouting at him, "wake up, Brethren! Wake up, you are in the midst of your enemies! This is no time to think of anything! Wake up!"

As if Brethren had been waiting for that jack, he grabs his sword and the shield. Soon he is fully prepared for the battle.

"Stand attention," Obedience commanded.

Brethren obeys

"Now," he continues, singing.

Onward redeemed solders!
Marching as to war!

With Promise, Patience, Obedience and other soldiers of Comforter around, Brethren is set to march into the midst of the enemies. He is ready to crush any number of enemies that come his way with one blow of his weapon of war.

With the influence of Patience, Obedience, Courage and Wisdom, more Conquerors team up with Brethren after he shares his experience and visions with them. They come together as one. The force becomes so formidable that while one person is chasing one thousand enemies at a time, two are putting ten thousand into flight. The enemies quickly retreat to recover from the fatal injuries, which they sustain. But then, the retreat is just for a while as Wickedness would not tolerate any of his armies taking a break.

The armies of Uncleanness launch their attack against some

Congregations, making a lot of redeemed people to either stain or remove the garments of Righteousness. This invariably grieves Comforter. He is so grieved that he leaves many redeemed people without warning or notice. As soon as he leaves, Emotion comes from Wickedness to replace him in their midst. Although some of their Captains try to put things right with the sword but it is too late. The enemies have penetrated the Congregations, making the people to gang up against them and throw them. They appoint other Captains who are willing to do what they want. Compromise takes over the leadership. The people are encouraged to make money in dirty ways as long as they give ten percent of it to the Captains. Instead of being clothed with garment of Righteousness so that they could be effective with the use of the armour, they dress so indecently that many people, including their Captains, get involved in sexual malpractice. There are female warriors of Wickedness called the Jezebels who appear in different forms and sizes. Some dress to suit the tastes of their victims but they are always equipped by Temptations and Seductions which they always use to open doors for warriors like Fornication, Adultery and Whoremongers to invade so many Congregations. They know the strength of each Congregations and how to wreck havoc in the lives of carefree redeemed people.

Captain Faithful is moved by Comforter to go from one Congregation to another to remind the people of what The Redeemer told them. "The redeemed people are now going wayward!" he said in one of the Congregations one day. "You cannot distinguish some redeemed people from the prostitutes in Bondage because of the way they dress. You cannot see the difference between a thief from some so-called-redeemed people who make money in such a dirty and dishonest way. What is the Congregation turning to? Check the words of The Redeemer and see if you're still his followers. I am not judging you but the words that will be used to judge every one of us is right with us. If the law says the person that kicks against the word of The Redeemer shall end up in Doom, you don't need any judge to tell you you're going to end up in Doom if you don't obey the word. The word of The

Redeemer happens to be the map that will guide us to Eternity. It is mirror for us to see if we are still in his likeness. It is the food that will preserve our souls until we get to Eternity. It is water of life that satisfies our thirst in this battlefield! It is the rod and the staff that comfort and direct us in the right path. It is hammer that will hit you when you're going wrong. It is the only sword we must use to fight the enemies. The word is our lives. Through the word we can have Comforter operating through us. Without it, we'll all be dead. The word is the mighty power that gives us victory upon victories, deliverance upon deliverance. The word of The Redeemer is The Redeemer himself. No matter what the enemies take from you, don't let them take the word of The Redeemer from you. If they succeed taking the word from you, you are dead even though it may look as if you are still alive. So you must meditate on the word, use it as a light that will guide you in the way you should walk in the kingdom that is full of darkness. Use it everyday and it shall be well with your soul. Don't follow the wrong way just because many are walking in it but rather follow the word of The Redeemer. Many people wear garments of Unrighteousness like barge of honour. What a shame! We are supposed to wear the armour of The Redeemer with pride because we are Conquerors! Let deaths and sufferings be our medals for doing the will of The Redeemer. When we get to Eternity, we shall show him how much we have suffered for him. Be ready to sacrifice any part of your bodies for his sake. If you lose a hand while fighting in the battlefield, that is a great honour for you. When you get to Eternity, The Redeemer will give you another hand with crowns that are made of pure gold. Then you will remember someone once told you that dying or suffering because of The Redeemer is the best way you can show to him that you love him. Do you love the Lord who died because to you? If you do, where is the proof? Is it in the riches you make in the kingdom at the expenses of people that are in Bondage and those who are perishing everyday in the battlefield? Is it the atrocities you commit day in day out that will show that you love him? Most of you have left the old love - the old way! You've turned into your own ways and yet you made people think you are redeemed. I just wonder at many of you. How are you going to explain to The Redeemer why you cannot get to Eternity after all he has done for us? Tell me! I don't care what you feel. I don't care what you will do to me for telling you the truth. But I tell you: all I'm saying had been kept as record in Eternity. It is meant to either save you from the snare of Wickedness or to be used against you on the day of judgment."

Despite all Captain Faithful said to the people, many still follow Ignorance who makes rooms for other armies of Wickedness to attack them at every side. The Jezebels continue to operate in Congregations, growing in popularity and using seductions and indecent dressings as weapons to influence the people. She introduces Indiscriminate Sex as one of the acquaintances of the people.

Temptations always looks for opportunities to take the battle from the Spirit into the Flesh. He does that through the Mind where Conquerors make decisions before doing anything. He always makes attempts to lure them from the Spirit to the Flesh where warriors of Wickedness could easily destroy them. The wise ones among the people know better than to fight their enemies in the Flesh, knowing fully well that they wrestle not against body and blood but against principalities and powers of Wickedness. They always take the battle to the Spirit where they have far better chances to defeat all their enemies, no matter how great they are.

Many of the redeemed people do not give room for Temptations to overcome them. They fight the warriors with powerful weapons of The Redeemer called Prayers and the sword, which can be used effectively in all the battlefields at all times. They use them so well that their enemies fall before them. As long as they do not allow Temptations to overcome them in the Flesh, they continue to claim victories over the enemies. They strictly adhere to what The Redeemer has commanded them through the mouth of faithful and fervent Captains that stand by The Word. Comforter takes over the lives of those who obey the words, directing all their affairs and teaching them how to use their armour effectively. With many soldiers of Comforter around them, they naturally become a chosen generation, a royal priesthood, a holy nation, a peculiar people who have obtained mercy from the Father. Knowledge Of The Word keeps reminding them the words of The Redeemer, which says, "dearly beloved, I beseech you as strangers and pilgrims, abstain from fleshly Lusts, which war against the soul."

The armies of Wickedness avoid such people. They just watch them as they rescue some of their slaves with the help of Comforter and the use of the amour. Although the enemies look for ways to strike or weaken them but the people are very careful. Comforter constantly exposes the secrets of the enemies to them. So the worst Wickedness could do is to send Fear to roar like a lion that walks about, looking as if he would devour. The enemies lament that they have short time to get as many people as possible to the bottomless pit before The Redeemer comes for his people. They are filled with fury and frustrations because so many redeemed people seem familiar with their plans and strategies.

The fight continues for a long time with some losing and some winning. The redeemed people that keep winning begin to have more people coming to join them. As they come together, they shoot countless number of arrows that carry fire at Wickedness and his warriors. The more they team up, the more powerful they become. The battle begins to get too fierce for Wickedness. Casualties become a regular occurrence among his warriors. Unable to withstand the agony any more, he quickly calls for an emergency meeting with his warriors. He knows they must design another strategy to deal with the redeemed people. If they do not do something very drastic about the indomitable forces of redeemed people, they would not only succeed in setting all the slaves free, they would also take the kingdom from him.

CHAPTER NINE

King Wickedness sits on his throne with his army officers sitting round him. He is holding some papers where he had scribbled his new plans. He has sketched out the ways to destroy the redeemed people once and for all.

After glancing through the papers, he clears his throat and looks at his officers. There are so many of them now. He has recruited as many warriors as are able to lead in the war. The newly recruited army officers are called Criticisms, Modernization, Worldliness, Self-Reliance, Denominationalism, Destructive Technology, Individualism, Disunity, Ambition, Self Glory, Prayerlessness, Homosexuality, Lesbianism, Horoscope and Indifference. The most dangerous among the newly recruited officers is Disunity. He is one of the special officers of Wickedness and the Captain of many of the new warriors.

King Wickedness looks at his officers. "You are all welcome," he said, pretending as if all is well. He knows what most of them are going through in the battlefield. By now, each of the warriors has one ugly experience or the other to share but he has not called the meeting to listen to any tale of woes.

"I wouldn't like to take much of your time because we have limited time before The Redeemer comes to take his people. I must admit that you have been fighting for twenty-four hours a day but there is need to intensify our efforts to get the redeemed people. In fact, I want you to work forty-eight hours a day. I guess you know

90

what I mean."

Again, Wickedness glances at the paper in his hand. "I want us to quickly evaluate what we have achieved so far and what we have suffered." Then he begins to read what he wrote in the paper. "So far, we have been able to get many redeemed people and their Captains into the bottomless pit. We are able to do this because most of the defeated people are foolish enough to fight the battle with us in the Flesh. As you know, we are superior to them when it comes to fighting the battle in the Flesh. As many as we are able to get in the Flesh, we always disarmed. Once they are disarmed, they are dead. We don't border ourselves about them, no matter what they claim to be. Their case is like a hunter who goes about hunting for animals. After killing many animals, which he keeps in his bag, he doesn't border himself about them because they are already his. He concentrates all his efforts on the animals that are alive.

"There are many redeemed people who are injured in the Flesh but they survive because they are able to escape to the Spirit where they receive treatments through the help of Comforter. Such people often go back to the rest and reveal our secret plans. Some who are still blind despite the injuries they sustain fall into our trap the second time and, of course, this gives our armies the opportunity to shoot more fiery darts at them. The people are now in the bottomless pit.

"I must not fail to tell you that I am aware of the injuries you have all suffered but you must remember that this is war. So injuries and deaths are common song we hear from both parties involved in the battle. Many redeemed people are very effective with their weapons of war. They are powerful enough to deal with many of our armies with their swords. Most of the fiery darts that are shot at them are quenched with their shields, which they hold with their strong bold hands. What particularly gives them victories is the involvement of soldiers of Comforter in the warfare. These mysterious soldiers who always flock with the Conquerors make each of them appears as if we are dealing with multitudes of enemies. The people never miss their target when they follow Comforter's leading. Nearly every time our armies gather to launch an attack, the courageous ones among the redeemed people often make an offensive move against us, throwing all our armies in disarray and putting them into the state of confusion with their dangerous weapons of war. A more devastating attack against our kingdom is the constant rescues of the slaves who always join the team of warring Conquerors. Many Conquerors take it as a point of duty to always set our slaves free even if it would cost them their lives. There are many remarkable incidents that convince me that some Conquerors are determined to wreck our kingdom just as we are determined to destroy theirs. I don't really have much time to give you the details of all that has happened but I will tell you briefly one of them.

"There are certain organizations working indirectly with us. These organizations always pretend to be redeemed people. A large number of people in the organizations sincerely believe that they are Conquerors but the truth is that they are not. I purposely allowed these organizations to be set up to fool our slaves who so much want to join the redeemed people.

"This incident I want to refer to happens in one of the organizations that belong to us. A member meets a Conqueror who wins him over to The Redeemer after making him see the difference between the organizations and the real redeemed people.

"The Conqueror later hands the man to Comforter who directs his ways. When the new convert gets back to his organization, he begins to cause trouble in the place. He tells the people bluntly that they had been fooled. With the help of Comforter and his soldiers, a large number of people in the organization are liberated from our kingdom."

Wickedness looks round at his officers who are so many that they cannot be counted. They are dead silent.

"Now you see how dangerous the redeemed people are in our midst," Wickedness says to them. "A soldier of The Redeemer who effectively uses his weapon can turn our kingdom upside down with the help of Comforter and his soldiers if we are not careful. To create more enemies that can constitute a disaster in our kingdom, all the follower of The Redeemer needs to do is to go to the slaves and convert them into followers. From the reports I have received from our armies, Conquerors are really wrecking a lot of havoc in our kingdom. The situation is so bad that we must not rejoice if we are able to get hundreds or thousands of them into the bottomless pit. For everyone we get into the pit, we lose at least three slaves from our kingdom. We all need to tighten our belts and fight to the finish." Wickedness sighs regretfully.

There is a long uncomfortable silence. All the warriors know that Wickedness is fast losing hope of gaining victories over the redeemed people.

Then Disunity stands and shouts, "we can disorganize the Conquerors! We can make them fight one another!"

Wickedness looks at him with his eyes looking bright with new hope. He gestures eagerly at Disunity as he asks excitedly, "how?"

Disunity smiles, walking round the people with patronizing stare. "Although I'm a new member in this army but I've been operating a long time." He pauses to look round at the officers. "If you check what The Redeemer told his people, he made mention of me. I am the most dangerous enemy of redeemed people and The Redeemer himself knows it."

He smiles again, nodding. "I am dangerous because I am an invisible warrior. Say invisible warrior!"

All the warriors, including Wickedness hail him. "Invisible warrior!"

Disunity gestures them to keep silence. Then he says, "I am also capable of appearing like soldier of Comforter like Open Rebuke, Discipline and anything I like. I was hoping this opportunity to prove my prowess will come one day. I didn't know it would come so soon. This is what I have in mind. I will go into the Congregations of our enemies. I will begin to cause disorderliness. With the help of Denominationalism, Legality, Creed, Individualism, Accusations, Ritualism and Religiosity; we can divide and rule them. We will always strike their Captains and make them to be at loggerheads. When we strike the Shepard, the flocks will scatter. Once they are scattered, we can rule them. Once we are ruling them, other armies can come into the Congregations and use them to fight one another. We can choose to destroy them if we like."

There is a sudden uproar of joy among the warriors. All the armies are so happy and impressed that they shake hands with Disunity for the brilliant idea.

"Now, now, now," Wickedness says, feeling very happy once again. He seems to have recovered his full strength. "We are getting somewhere." He regroups all the armies. Being the deadliest enemy of the redeemed people, he places Disunity as the head. By the virtue of his new position, Disunity automatically became the field marshal. None of the armies complains because all the warriors know he deserves the position. Besides, Wickedness has so disciplined his armies that they never envy one another. In fact, as soon as a leader is appointed, no one would complain even if he is a child or an amateur or a mediocre. To them, a leader is a leader and they are always obliged to team up with him.

With the new appointment of the leader of the warriors, the meeting ended.

Field Marshal Disunity pays official visits to each Congregation of redeemed people without any visible appearance. His target is to stir conflicts among the Captains who are directing all the affairs of the Congregations. While the Captains are having a meeting in one of the strongest Congregations on how to launch an attack against Wickedness and how to rescue the people in Bondage, Disunity sits among the people and begins to look for opportunity to disorganize them. He knows he wouldn't have to wait for so long before he is given the chance to strike.

CHAPTER TEN

One of the Captains presiding over the meeting said, "now, you all know we have lost so much people. You can imagine how The Redeemer will feel about that. He doesn't want to lose anybody. All the same, while lamenting over the people we have lost, we can consider the people that had been added to us. Many people are coming to know The Redeemer. We have truly become the light of the people in the kingdom. Many have come to know the truth. We thank The Redeemer for giving us Comforter who tells us what to say or do to the people in Bondage and how to use our weapons.

"I call this meeting in order to evaluate what we have accomplished so far, reinforce and equip our troops." He paused briefly before he continued, "many of our people, especially those who newly join us don't know how to fight. So instead of taking them to the battlefield, we need to equip them with the armours and the word of The Redeemer. Unless that, they may not be able to face the enemies. There is remarkable difference between the Conquerors and the redeemed people. While the Conquerors fight against the enemies, the followers are like babes who still need to be fed with milk. As you all know that it is not right to take babes to field, we don't send the followers to fight just like that even though they are potential Conquerors. We have to groom them first. Even then, each time the enemies besiege our Congregations; we always lose a lot of followers. The Conquerors have to fend for

95

themselves as well as the followers. So there is every chance to lose followers who are not equipped by Knowledge Of The Word when deadly warriors like Ignorance and Fear attack. I now feel the need to call this meeting to talk about how to build more Conquerors that will launch steady and constant attack against the enemies. We also need to talk about making the followers to become Conquerors as soon as possible before we lose them to Wickedness. If all the redeemed people are Conquerors, we need not to feel so much concern about losing anyone. But a follower cannot be a Conqueror immediately. In fact, there are some followers who lose their lives everyday because they think they are good enough to withstand the enemies. And that reminds me of the words of The Redeemer which says that he that thinks he stands should take heed or else he falls. As we can see now, it is not even enough to stand. We must fight. I, therefore, want us all to suggest a way of building followers into Conquerors and how to launch steady attack against the Wickedness without losing anyone among our people."

One of the Captains called Captain Doctrines said, "let's make it a point of duty for every follower of The Redeemer to conform to the principle of restitution before he can become part of us. For instance, if any of them has done anything that is contrary to what the Lord told us, he must put it right. In doing so, followers would be getting built into Conquerors."

"No," another leader called Captain Stern said. "The principle of restitution is not in line with what the Lord said. The Lord said that if a slave that is set free from Bondage follows his statutes, all the contrary things he has done would not be mentioned unto him. Besides, he made us realized that if we are converted to his side, all things have become new. It is as if the person has done nothing wrong."

"What would you say of someone who steals some things and is still in possession of that thing?" Captain Doctrine asked, trying to establish his point. "You know the Lord always want us to do things right. Take for instance, sometimes ago when one of our people did something wrong while going to Promised Land, the wrong act cause the enemies to defeat the people. When the leader of the people sought for the reason for the defeat, it was discovered that one of the people called Achan had stolen accursed thing. He kept it in his stuff. Because of that, the people of the Lord could not stand before their enemies. It was after the thing Achan had stolen had been removed that they were able to face the enemies again." He looked round at the people. "With this fact, there is need to establish the principle of restitution. That is one of the things we must use to build the followers into Conquerors."

Captain Stern looked irritated as he said, "you're making the statutes of the Lord contradict one another. The Lord said we are justified to be his people by our faith in him, not by works. Besides, as he said, by the deeds of the law shall no flesh be justified in his sight, but we are justified by his grace."

"Now, now," Captain Doctrine said, "what are you suggesting? Do you mean that thieves in Bondage should be accommodated with theirs loots?"

"What I'm suggesting is that everything we have to do must be done as Comforter suggests. He knows every word of the Lord and what they mean."

"I'm sure Comforter will not suggest that someone who wishes to be a follower of The Redeemer should keep what is not his," Captain Doctrine said.

"Perhaps you can explain what can be done if he had gotten rid of the thing," Captain Stern said.

"He might have to pay for it!" Captain Doctrine said. "Everything he stole would have to be paid for."

"What do you say of a murder case, Captain Doctrine?" Captain Stern asked, looking steadily at him. "How do you expect a murderer to bring the person he has killed back to live?"

"I'm not talking of the things outside his ability to do?"

"Then what do you mean?" Captain Stern asked, pleased with himself.

"Well," Captain Doctrine said, "I mean things he has the ability to put right."

"Man!" Captain Stern said in irritation, "you mustn't heap

97

unnecessary loads on the heads of people for coming to The Redeemer. If we have to put right every wrong thing we have done, we'll spend the rest of our lives doing that. Besides, we make the word of the Lord that says we are justified freely by his grace through the redemption from Wickedness of no effect."

"I disagree!" Captain Doctrine flared up.

"Now that's enough," one of the other Captains called Concern said, "we must not fight over little things like restitution."

Captain Doctrine said, "that's not little to me. So I'm setting up my own Congregations with my own people unless you accept the application of restitution."

All the Captains began to look at one another in the face. Of course, no one saw Disunity sitting among them, making all the people felt differently.

"Are you accepting the principle or not?" Captain Doctrine asked.

"I'm not," Captain Stern said.

"Well, we already have two different groups now," Captain Doctrine said, looking at the rest. "Which one are you supporting?'

Some of the Captains took Captain Doctrine's side while some take sides with Stern.

Captain Doctrine with the Captains that supported him and some followers who also believed that everybody must put right all the wrong things he or she has done left the Congregations to pitch their tent in another place. With that, Disunity succeeded in dividing one of the most powerful Congregations that were wrecking havoc in the kingdom of Wickedness.

Of course, field marshal Disunity is not through with the redeemed people yet. He sits with another Captain called Sceptic at the meeting in another Congregation.

"Now," Captain Old Time, one of the leaders in the Congregation says, "so many things are going wrong now. We no long yield to what Comforter says."

"Comforter is no longer in the Congregations." Captain Sceptic says. "The time Comforter was present has gone."

Captain Old Time looks surprised. "What do you mean by

saying he is gone? He just spoke to me yesterday."

"You lied, you know;" Captain Skeptic says. "I know Comforter is gone because he's no longer operating. He left shortly after the Lord has gone."

"If you say Comforter is gone," Captain Old Time says, "who is warning us of the danger ahead of us, who had been leading us? Who had …?"

"Those are works of emotion and human perceptions, not works of Comforter. You know as well as everyone does that we've been working around here without Comforter."

"You speak for yourself, Captain Skeptic," Captain Old Time says. "I believe Comforter is very much with us since the Lord gave him to us. He had been operating in our midst. Only those who are familiar with him can perceive his presence. If you don't believe he is with us, that's your own creed; not mine."

"You better face the fact that all our activities, including yours are man-made. We all know how it works…"

"I'm not here to argue with you," Captain Old Time interrupts. "But you must realize that Comforter had been with us, no matter what you say or think. The mere fact that you don't believe Comforter is around is enough reason to think you've been fighting the battle in the Flesh."

"Wherever you think of me, I don't care. I know one thing for sure. I'm better fighter than you."

"I wonder how you can make a good fighter without Comforter. Anyone with Comforter by his side is far better than you, no matter how small he is."

"What you said just now makes a lot of difference between the two of us," Captain Skeptic says with annoyance. "I believe in facing the truth. The truth is: you have been working on the people's emotion, making them feel it was Comforter operating. Unless you let people know the fact that Comforter is gone, we will have to part ways."

"Why should I deny Comforter after all I've experienced about him?" Captain Old Time says impatiently.

"Keep fooling yourself about Comforter. I'm out of here,"

Captain Skeptic says. "I'm leaving the Congregation with people who believe the fact that Comforter is no longer around."

"Before you leave, Captain Skeptic," Captain Old Time says, feeling sorry that he was going to lead many people into Doom. "I might have to remind you of what the Lord said about praying to the Father to give us Comforter who will abide with us for ever. Since you admit that Comforter had come to the Congregation, do you think the Lord will change his mind by calling him back? He said he'd stay with us forever. That means he'll stay with us till the Lord comes for us."

"The Lord can change his mind if sin is too much," Captain Skeptic says. "Remember what he says about grieving Comforter. Comforter left because the people grieved him."

"Comforter cannot just leave us like that just because one or more people grieve him, especially when he knows how much we need him. Believe me, there is no way we can win the battle against Wickedness without him."

"Blab, blab, jab, jab," Captain Skeptic says indifferently. "Go tell that to someone who believes in stuff like that. I don't."

With that, Skeptic leaves the Congregations to pitch his tent with some followers in another place.

Field Marshal Disunity is very happy with himself. By now, all the armies of Wickedness are beginning to have a great deal of respect for him. With Disunity operating in all the Congregations without any visible appearance, the redeemed people begin to bear grudges against one another, killing one another with mouths. This makes them to grow weak. Very few are strong enough to deal heavy blow against warriors of Wickedness. Mainly because the people no longer cooperate with one another, they cannot tackle the enemies like before. They always suspect any Conquerors who have good intention to let them see the need to come together. The division so much affects the body of The Redeemer that instead of two Conquerors to chase ten thousand enemies at the same time, one is chasing one thousand at different times. The operation of Disunity brings about the worst defeat in the history of redeemed people. It gives their enemies better chance to oppress them in the Flesh, in the Mind and even in the Spirit where they are supposed to be victorious.

Captain Concern, Faith, Brethren and many other Captains studied the situation carefully and look up in despair. "Oh, Lord," they mutter within themselves. "What's happening?" They can hardly see field Marshal Disunity sitting in their midst. He causes some of the Captains to disagree on the administration of the Congregations. They disagree on the way the followers should live and dress. They disagree on what each Congregation should believe. They disagree on finances. They disagree on whether females should teach others about the word of The Redeemer or not. They argue whether females can head Congregations or not. They disagree on the day the people should hear the words of The Redeemer. They disagree on how to discipline erring follower of The Redeemer. They disagree on virtually everything. No one has respect for the opinions of others because of the presence of Disunity in their midst. They do not see the reason to come together again as one because of the differences in opinions, values, backgrounds, races, creeds, cultures, ethnic groups, social status, family heritages, Congregations and understanding of the words of The Redeemer. Disunity uses warriors like Criticism, Denominationalism and other warriors to make the people fight one another. They are divided into many groups at the end of each passing day. There are always so many different groups of Congregations. The divisions are so much that even within a Congregation there are different groups of people who are constantly at loggerheads with one another.

The armies of Disunity invade all the Congregations with full force. Individualism, Hypocrisies, Worldliness, Idolatry that always appears in a subtle and friendly way, Fashion, High minds, Uncleanness, Legalism, Apostasy join other warriors at various Congregations to strike many of the redeemed people dead.

The redeemed people no longer co-operate with one another. When a follower of The Redeemer sees another follower fighting the enemies, he would first like to know which Congregation he belongs before he considers helping him. If he is not a member of his Congregation, he would simply fold his arm and watch the enemy destroying the follower. With this type of attitude, the enemies are able to destroy uncountable number of redeemed people. If the follower is destroyed, he would conclude, 'he is destroyed because he belongs to the wrong Congregation.'

Grieved with sorrow, Captain Concern sits in a lonely place one day, wondering where Comforter who is supposed to guide the redeemed people has gone. He begins to shed much tears, feeling his heart breaking into pieces. He remembers the emphasis The Redeemer had laid on unity and he remembers how he has felt so sorrowful before he departed, saying, "will I still find faith among you when I return?" He knows now why he had felt so sorrowful and he wonders if he had foreseen this happening.

Suddenly he groans in a loud voice, "oh Lord! How long shall the wicked, how long shall the wicked triumph? How long shall they utter and speak bad things? And all the workers of iniquities boast themselves? They break in pieces thy people, O Lord, and afflict thine heritage. They slay the widow and the stranger and murder the fatherless. Who will rise up for us against the workers of iniquities? Unless the Lord had been our help, our souls have almost dwelt in silence. When we said, our feet slippeth, thy mercy, O Lord help us up!"

After groaning for a long time, he falls into silence. In the dead silence, Comforter whispers, "Concern, my people perish because they lack knowledge of the things that is happening around them. They have no spiritual eyes and they forget things so easily. Worst of all, they are disobedient to the words of The Redeemer. They forsake the way of The Redeemer and walk after their own imagination. They trust in their understanding and refuse to take my counsel. I give them Wisdom, Knowledge Of The Word and Understanding, the principal soldiers that can help them overcome a lot of their enemies but they would rather use their initiatives to do things their own ways. I warn them of the danger in not listening to me but they don't yield to me. When they disobey me, I have to forsake them. I decide to stay with only those who will listen to me. Because I am not around them, the enemies get into their midst without anyone seeing it.

"I will reveal to you the secret behind this to you. There is a special army commander of Wickedness called Disunity. He is the one that disorganizes all of you. He uses divide and rule tactics to control most of the people. Wickedness has a lot of tactics, which I would have readily revealed to you only if all of you stick together as one, but the most effective and destructive of all is the divide and rule tactics. The Redeemer knows that the battle would come to this level. So he gives you a commandment that you should not grieve me. I would have tolerated all of you, using one person to teach another, if you have given my soldier called Love the chance to operate but most of you kick him out in the cold where he is made to freeze. You were all instructed to let Love dwell with all of you but you broke that golden rule. If you have let Love to dwell with you, nothing would have separated you. Because you don't, Disunity is able to get into your midst to weaken and disarm most of you."

"Comforter," Concern says, "you are supposed to direct the people. You should have warned the people before hand."

"They were told," Comforter replies. "The early redeemed people even practiced the golden rule by having all things in common. They believed that they were of one heart and of one soul. That gave them so much victory. Since the people gave Disunity room to operate, the enemies have no problem dealing with you."

"But Comforter," Concern says, "what must I do so that the people don't perish before the Lord comes?"

"Like I indicated," Comforter says, "the people will not listen to you. They would think you want to re-organize and rule them. They will not understand your good intention to help them. They have been blind folded. Besides, their Captains feed them with so much creeds that they would rather take to the creed of their Congregations than to heed what The Redeemer told them."

"Oh, no!" cries Concern helplessly. "Surely, there's something I can do. Comforter, please, instruct me to do something anything. There must be some people out there that

103

would listen to me. With your help, I know they will listen to me. It's better than doing nothing. I can't stand this defeat and shame any more. Something must be done!"

"Well," Comforter says, "I can only commission you to do the little you can by telling everybody the truth about what the enemies is doing in their lives. Share with them the message I have given you. I will convince those who want to know that truth that I send you the message. Whatever you tell them will either be used to transform them or kept as a record that would be used against them on the day of judgment. He who has ears among them will hear. And he who has no ears will not hear until he finds himself in Doom. After all, a falcon that will get lost will not hear the falconer."

Then there is dead silence. Concern knows that he has great task to tell everybody all he had received as a message from Comforter.

EPILOGUE

WHAT IS THIS ALL ABOUT?

This is a message about Jesus Christ, you, me, the people all over the world, Satan and his spirit servants. Jesus gave us himself so that we may be free. He doesn't have to die but he died anyway. Even though he is God, he took the form of man and offered himself as atonement for the sins, which we commit. He fought the battle in hell, which we cannot fight. He took the key from Satan who held everybody in captive and set us free. He gave us freedom but everybody knows it was not cheap. It cost him his life, blood and dignity. He did not mind that because he loves us. He was not comfortable to see what was happening to mankind. So he has to come down from heaven to redeem us. When he was on earth, he was not even recognized as God and the Messiah. He looked at those who believed in him with compassion because we are like sheep without a shepherd.

"And Jesus, when he came out, saw much people, and was moved with compassion toward them, because they were as sheep not having a shepherd: and he began to teach them many things." Mark 6:34

Everybody is going his own way, not minding the truth that we are all heading to our doom. So he came down to make our way straight. Yes, he came down and set us free. When he completed his mission on earth, the Scriptures say in John 19:30,

105

"When Jesus therefore had received the vinegar, he said, It is finished: and he bowed his head, and gave up the ghost."

Yes, truly, it is finished. He has established the truth on earth. He knows that there is need to know this truth before anyone can be free indeed. We need to know this truth because there is everything we need in the truth. We read in John 8:32 that:

"And ye shall know the truth, and the truth shall make you free."

In John 14:6, the Bible says,

Jesus saith unto him, I am the way, the truth, and the life: no man cometh unto the Father, but by me."

Jesus will set you free if you know him because he is the way, the truth and the life.

He is the greatest and most wonderful gift God has ever given us. In Isaiah 9:6, the Bible says,

For unto us a child is born, unto us a son is given: and the government shall be upon his shoulder: and his name shall be called Wonderful, Counsellor, The mighty God, The everlasting Father, The Prince of Peace."

It is the true picture of Jesus that is painted in the Bible, the Word of God. It is by truth that we live and survive. Everything about our lives depends on this truth. In truth, we are delivered. In truth, we are assured of eternity. In truth we are protected against the enemies. In truth, we wage war and in truth, believers are conquerors. In fact, our freedom and victories depend on the whole truth we know. Needless to say, not knowing the whole truth is enough to make the enemies to oppress a believer. Because Jesus knows that we need the whole truth before we can become conquerors, he gave us Holy Spirit, Comforter to teach all things. Jesus said in John 14:26,

"But the Comforter, which is the Holy Ghost, whom the Father will send in my name, he shall teach you all things, and bring all things to your remembrance, whatsoever I have said unto you."

To be a Conqueror, we need the whole armour of God. The Bible has this to say in Ephesians 6:12-13,

"For we wrestle not against flesh and blood, but against principalities, against powers, against the rulers of the darkness of this world, against spiritual wickedness in high places.

Wherefore take unto you the whole armour of God, that ye may be able to withstand in the evil day, and having done all, to stand."

We need to know the truth about our enemies who, as the names connote in the story, are not flesh and blood. They are the cause of perversion of the truth about salvation and the change of Christianity into religious activities. As already indicated in the story, he fights both Christians and non-Christians through their flesh, in the spirit realm and in their minds. He not only makes people follow the wrong way but also pervert the truth in order to lead astray. This is a tactic of deceptions before total destructions. There is need for everybody to know the truth about the enemy. The Bible says of him in John 10:10,

The thief cometh not, but for to steal, and to kill, and to destroy...."

He has so many warriors that help him to carry out these three deadly missions and he has far too many tactics of dealing with Christians. He knows individual's weak areas and the best way to deal with each believer. He fights the spiritual battle with us, using so many things; including fellow human beings and things of this world as weapons. The word of God says in 1 Peter 5:8-9,

"Be sober, be vigilant; because your adversary the devil, as a roaring lion, walketh about, seeking whom he may devour:
"Whom resist steadfast in the faith, knowing that the same afflictions are accomplished in your brethren that are in the world."

As you can see in the story, nobody is invulnerable to the attack of the enemy of mankind. His attack is more against believers. The stronger a Christian, the severe the attack. The weaker the Christian, the less the devil or his servants pay attention to him or her. In fact, the moment a person becomes born-again, he declares him wanted in his kingdom.

He makes life miserable for believers, knowing fully well that God has prepared a place for them in Eternity, the place that is full of nothing but bliss. The Bible says in Revelation 21:4,

"And God shall wipe away all tears from their eyes; and there shall be no more death, neither sorrow, nor crying, neither shall there be any more pain: for the former things are passed away."

Another point I want you to get in the story is that all evils originate from the devil. They are organized and initiated by him and his servants, which are uncountable. If the spirits of the devil are removed from the life of a person, you will see the original image, which God has created in him. The truth is: most people do not know who the real enemy is. The enemy takes advantage of this ignorance to fight them with what they can see. He uses ungodly films, television programs, music and even publications; including books to fight the battle in their minds. Anyone who attempts to educate such people about all these would be considered fanatics. Who would believe that things that serve as means of entertainment, information and education had become ideal tools which the enemy can use to make people neglect Christ except they are sound spiritually. If so many Christians find it hard to understand the methods the enemy uses to fight them, making them to conform to the standard of this world, how then can others who are yet to come to the knowledge of Christ comprehend the challenges in Christianity? So many people now find this world a pleasant place to stay. So they no longer aspire to be in the presence of the Lord. Those who study the trend of the world understand that the devil has made it a terrible place to stay. Only visions to do the will of God can make this world convenient to dwell. The Bible says in Proverbs 29:18-20 of vision,

"Where there is no vision, the people perish: but he that keepeth the law, happy is he.

"A servant will not be corrected by words: for though he understand he will not answer.

"Seest thou a man that is hasty in his words? there is more hope of a fool than of him."

Because so many people lack the visions about God, His kingdom and salvation, so many Churches have now graduated from compromise into worldliness. Through the operations of the enemy, some are going from worldliness into idolatry by laying more emphasis on material things than things of eternal values.

Now you have an idea of the operations of the enemy who is working tirelessly to lead many people into destruction, what are you doing with the weapon God has given you to fight back, to defend yourself and to rescue people that are ignorantly and innocently walking to hell everyday? The Bible says in 2 Corinthians 10:4-5,

"For the weapons of our warfare are not carnal, but mighty through God to the pulling down of strong holds;

Casting down imaginations, and every high thing that exalteth itself against the knowledge of God, and bringing into

109

captivity every thought to the obedience of Christ;"

As you have read it in the story, it is not enough to have the power and the weapon to fight the devil and his servants, your knowledge also matters. What you know about the word of God and how willing you are to apply the word will determine if you will be victorious. It is true that Christians are more than conquerors for the Bible say so in Romans 8:37-39. It must be realized that, no matter how difficult it is to keep Christian sanity in this morally insane world, high level of discipline on the part of every believer is required to be victorious even though the Holy Spirit will make up for what we do not have the power to control. Through the battles you have won, you know you are a Conqueror and through the battles you have lost, you know your weakness. Each battle you win makes you more of a Conqueror until you are more than a Conqueror. Moreover, you can only claim to be Conqueror after going through chains of battles that will never end until you depart from this world. Jesus points out this fact in Matthew 10:22,

"And ye shall be hated of all men for my name's sake: but he that endureth to the end shall be saved."

Christians have all the chances to win all the battles they fight. The question, however, is why are so many defeated? The reason is that they have replaced the word of God with creeds and human ideas. Many Christians now think, talk, dance, dress, sing, walk and behave like people of the world in the name of modern ways of life and yet they want to be victorious. They are no longer the people the Bible called peculiar people and they do not behave as royal priesthood. They are longer serve as the light of the world because their weapons of warfare have become burdensome. It no longer matters to them to pray and live holy life. Their lives are no longer epistles, which men can read. The Bible says in 2 Corinthians 3:1-3,

"Do we begin again to commend ourselves? or need we, as some others, epistles of commendation to you, or letters of commendation from you?

"Ye are our epistle written in our hearts, known and read of all men:

"Forasmuch as ye are manifestly declared to be the epistle of Christ ministered by us, written not with ink, but with the Spirit of the living God; not in tables of stone, but in fleshy tables of the heart."

It is hard to read the word of God in the lives of many believers nowadays. Christianity is no longer a way of life in modern days but a fashionable thing to do. Most do not know that being born-again means more than what they say but also what they do, what they think, their lifestyles, what they eat or drink and what they wear. The Bible says in Romans 14:17,

"For the kingdom of God is not meat and drink; but righteousness, and peace, and joy in the Holy Ghost."

Most people do not seem to appreciate that Christianity is a yoke of our Lord Jesus - the cross. If a Christian does not take the cross, which comes in the forms of the challenges he faces everyday, or in the temptations to compromise, the enemy will give him the yoke that is eternally destructive though it may seem like great conveniences. With the comfort of the Holy Spirit, the cross will seem like a light thing. Jesus says in Matthew 11:29-30,

Take my yoke upon you, and learn of me; for I am meek and lowly in heart: and ye shall find rest unto your souls.
For my yoke is easy, and my burden is light.

There is no way anyone can bear the enormous responsibilities that go along with being a Christian without the help of the Holy Spirit. Without him, there is no way anyone can carry the yoke or reflect the image of Christ. Many people have discarded the presence of the Holy Spirit in their lives. So holiness has become a dead issue. Righteousness - right standing with God has become old fashion. Many assume that God has lowered His standard of righteousness. And so they feel others who are actually practicing Christianity are just being fanatical. If man would find it difficult to change his constitution, which he uses to enforce orderliness in his environment, how then can anyone expect God to reduce the yardstick He had used to measure the righteousness of the early Christians? God would be unjust if He changes His word to suit the purpose of the present day people or because they cannot meet up. Believe me, God will never change His word for any reason. So what is in the Bible, His word, is what He is going to use to judge everybody; no matter your status, race, Church creed, principle or policy or background.

Now you know the problem with individual Christians and weapon of warfare, what is happening to the Church? She is divided into many denominations. Even then, denominationalism is not the real problem. The real problem is disunity after the divisions into denominations. Many denominations are claiming to be superior to the others. Instead of praying for and teaching others that are departing from the word, they are exhibiting the attitudes of holier-than-thou or more-knowledgeable-than-thou. They are helping the enemies to achieve their aims without knowing it. They are doing the work of the Lord out of strife, not with genuine and sincere hearts. They preach condemnations instead of teaching the truth with love. Some leaders who actually need the help of others in their ministries will not be humble enough to ask for it. Hence, the congregation would be denied of the sound doctrine that can help the spiritual growths of the people. Some would not honour the invitations to teach believers in another Church because they do not belong to the same denomination. Hence the Churches that are full of babes would not be given the privilege to benefits from other teachers of the word of God.

I heard a preacher whom I respect so much attributing to himself all the gifts in the Body of Christ. He claimed to be a prophet, evangelist, teacher and whatever. So he hardly needed anyone to help him in his ministries. I just wonder at the number of people like that. The Bible has something to say about this in 1 Corinthians 12:4-12,

"Now there are diversities of gifts, but the same Spirit.

"And there are differences of administrations, but the same Lord.

"And there are diversities of operations, but it is the same God which worketh all in all.

"But the manifestation of the Spirit is given to every man to profit withal.

"For to one is given by the Spirit the word of wisdom; to another the word of knowledge by the same Spirit;

"To another faith by the same Spirit; to another the gifts of healing by the same Spirit;

"To another the working of miracles; to another prophecy; to another discerning of spirits; to another divers kinds of tongues; to another the interpretation of tongues:

"But all these worketh that one and the selfsame Spirit, dividing to every man severally as he will.

"For as the body is one, and hath many members, and all the members of that one body, being many, are one body: so also is Christ."

Many leaders view their congregations in terms of numbers instead of individual person that must be nurtured. So they are concerned about figures going up. The Body of Christ is starved of the sound doctrines, causing the spiritual deaths of so many people of God. Some Church leaders are going as far as manipulating some people to fulfill their ambitions to excel in the material worlds. Because some Churches have failed to identify the type of calling of some people, they have given their leadership to the wrong ministers. Going by the story, there are three types of callings. Some are actually called by God, some by the devil and some are called by men or self-called. Even among those who are

113

called by God, many have failed to identify where God wants them to operate. In actual fact, every genuine Christian is called to serve but they need to know where God wants them to function. Just as there are military, air forces and navy; God has Conquerors assigned to various areas. Some are called to be teachers, some pastors or evangelists. Each of them can only be effective in the areas God have called him into. So many Churches have made the mistake of appointing wrong people to lead them. Often times, inexperienced people found themselves as leaders. As it is dangerous to place untrained soldier to command a troop, it is eternally disastrous to appoint an inexperienced person to lead or be placed in the ministry he is not called into.

I assume now that you understand all the problems the story has pointed out. So let us see what the Lord have got to say to all the Churches. To one Church in Ephesus, He said; "I know thy works and thy labour, and thy patience, and how thou canst not bear them which are evil: and thou hast tried them which say they are apostles and are not, and has found them liars. And hast borne, and hast patience, and for my name's sake hast laboured, and has not fainted. Nevertheless I have somewhat against thee, because thou hast left thy first love. Remember therefore from whence thou art fallen, and repent, and do the first works; or else I will come unto thee quickly, and remove thy candlestick out of his place, except thou repent." (Revelation 2:2-5)

He said to another Church in Smyrna, "I know thy works, and tribulation, and poverty (but thou art rich) and I know the blasphemy of them which say they are Jews and are not, but are the synagogue of Satan. Fear none of these things which thou shall suffer: behold the devil shall cast some of you into prison, that ye may be tried; and ye shall have tribulation ten days: be thou faithful into death, and I will give thee a crown of life." (Revelation 2:9-10)

To another church in Pergamos, the Lord said, "I know thy works and where thou dwellest, even where Satan's seat is: and thou holdest fast my name, and hast not denied my faith, even in those days wherein Antipas was my faithful Martyr, who was slain among thee, because thou has there them that hold the doctrine of Balaam who taught Balak to cast a stumbling block before the children of Israel to eat things sacrificed unto idols, and to commit fornication. So hast thou also them that hold the doctrine of Nicolaitaines which thing I hate. Repent; or else I will come unto thee quickly, and will fight against them with the sword of my mouth." (Revelation 2:13-16)

He said to another church in Thyatira, "I know thy works, and charity, and service, and faith and thy patience, and thy works; and the last to be more than the first. Notwithstanding I have a few things against thee, because thou sufferest that woman Jezebel, which calleth herself a prophetess, to teach and to seduce my servants to commit fornication, and to eat things sacrificed unto idols. And I gave her space to repent of her fornication; and she repented not. Behold, I will cast her into a bed, and them that commit adultery with her into great tribulation, except they repent of their deeds. And I will kill her children with death; and all the churches shall know that I am he which searcheth reins and hearts: and I will give unto everyone of you rest in Thyatira, as many as have not this doctrine, and which have not know the depths of Satan, as they speak; I will put upon you burden. But that which ye have already hold fast till I come. And he that overcometh, and keepeth my works unto the end, to him will give power over the nations." (Revelation 2: 19-26)

He said to another Church in Sardis, "Be watchful, and strengthen the things which remain, that are ready to die: for I have not found thy works perfect before God.

Remember therefore how thou hast received and heard, and hold fast, and repent. If therefore thou shalt not watch, I will come on thee as a thief, and thou shalt not know what hour I will come upon thee. Thou hast a few names even in Sardis which have not defiled their garments; and they shall walk with me in white: for they are worthy. He that overcometh, the same shall be clothed in white raiment; and I will not blot out his name out of the book of life, but I will confess his name before my Father, and before his angels." (Revelation 3:2-5)

115

He said to another church in Philadelphia, "And to the angel of the church in Philadelphia write; These things saith he that is holy, he that is true, he that hath the key of David, he that openeth, and no man shutteth; and shutteth, and no man openeth; I know thy works: behold, I have set before thee an open door, and no man can shut it: for thou hast a little strength, and hast kept my word, and hast not denied my name. Behold, I will make them of the synagogue of Satan, which say they are Jews, and are not, but do lie; behold, I will make them to come and worship before thy feet, and to know that I have loved thee. Because thou hast kept the word of my patience, I also will keep thee from the hour of temptation, which shall come upon all the world, to try them that dwell upon the earth. Behold, I come quickly: hold that fast which thou hast, that no man take thy crown. Him that overcometh will I make a pillar in the temple of my God, and he shall go no more out: and I will write upon him the name of my God, and the name of the city of my God, which is new Jerusalem, which cometh down out of heaven from my God: and I will write upon him my new name. (Revelation 3:7-12)

He said to another church in Laodiceans, "I know thy works, that thou art neither cold nor hot: I would thou wert cold or hot. So then because thou art lukewarm, and neither cold nor hot, I will spue thee out of my mouth. Because thou sayest, I am rich, and increased with goods, and have need of nothing; and knowest not that thou art wretched, and miserable, and poor, and blind, and naked: I counsel thee to buy of me gold tried in the fire, that thou mayest be rich; and white raiment, that thou mayest be clothed, and that the shame of thy nakedness do not appear; and anoint thine eyes with eyesalve, that thou mayest see. As many as I love, I rebuke and chasten: be zealous therefore, and repent. Behold, I stand at the door, and knock: if any man hear my voice, and open the door, I will come in to him, and will sup with him, and he with me. To him that overcometh will I grant to sit with me in my throne, even as I also overcame, and am set down with my Father in his throne. (Revelation 3:15-21)

What is the Lord telling you or your church? Well, He is

telling everybody, including you and me in Revelation 2:11, " He that hath ear let him hear what the Spirit saith unto the churched. He that overcometh shall not be hurt of the second death." The second death is interpreted in Revelation 21:8 as "...the lake which burneth with fire and brimstone...."115

CHECK OUT OTHER BOOKS BY DIPO TOBY ALAKIJA
Each Serves Either As Edifying Or Evangelical Or Missionary Or Academic Tool At Home, School, Bible Clubs, Sunday Schools, Church, Office And Other Fellowships

NO MORE TEARS TO SHED
ISBN: 978-49874-3-0 ISBN: 978-978-74-3-1

Kidnappers took Tokunbo away from his grand parents in a city in Nigeria when he was a little boy. A nice woman found him in another town and gave him a false identity. She spoilt him with love, making him to grow into a rebellious teenager that was not appreciated anywhere. When Janet made him a Christian, however, life began to make sense to him until the day he was beaten to the point of death for the offence he knew nothing about. He left the town for the city which, unknown to him, held his true identity and the link to his parents in the United States. To find them was only a question of time.

THE UNROMANTIC LOVE BIRDS
ISBN: 978-4987-5-7 ISBN: 978-978-4974-5-5

And other short stories about love and marriages

They were very much in love right from their school days but when they got married and had children, romance became the game Charles' wife refused to play. No matter how much he tried to make her understand the unbearable condition her unromantic attitude has subjected him into, she would not change. Consequently, after enduring for so long, he was forced to look for the women that would make up for her weakness. He unofficially married a beautiful lady of insane jealousy. Though she was ready to give him what was missing in his marriage, it soon dawn on him that he has solved one big problem only to create a bigger one.

BLOODSHED IN CAMPUS
ISBN: 978-07350-3-8 ISBN: 978-978-07350-3-6

A poor widow tearfully warned her son, Richard, against joining the bad wagon when he got an admission into one of the Nigerian Universities. He resisted the membership of groups of students, including the Christian Fellowship until he had an encounter with a member of The Black Skulls - a deadly and ruthless secret cult on the campus.

Before Richard knew what he was up against, the head of The Black Skulls had arranged items for his initiation into the cult. While resisting being initiated, he ran to the Christian Fellowship for help. The leader

118

of the Christian Fellowship dragged The President of Students' Union Government (S.U.G) into the conflict. With the involvement of the S.U.G President, another formidable cult called The Red Eyes felt obliged to team up against The Black Skulls. Then the campus turned into a battlefield and BLOODSHED became the order of the black day.

NETWORK BIBLE CLUB
YOUTH AND ADULT BOOK ONE
ISBN: 978 - 978- 49874-9-X ISBN: 978-978-49874-9-3
A collection of 26 life transforming stories, 26 poems, 26 hymn tuned songs and weekly Bible lessons

The issue of moral instructions in schools and at homes is threatened with extinction. Consequently, so many youths are involved in prostitution, drug addictions, cultism, fraudulent practices, armed robberies and other crimes. Those who are supposed to be trained as leaders in various walks of life are the ones posing serious threats to many lives. Many parents who fail to add moral values to the upbringing of their children often times breed potential criminals under their roofs without knowing it. Apart from these, many other people negatively influence young ones through the media, music, publications, films, conduct and foul language; making them to lose their moral and family values.

This book one just like the rest of other volumes is an attempt to bring back moral instructions into schools and campuses through the use of stories, hymn tuned songs, poems, Bible lessons and class activities. It is designed to assist teachers and ministers in Secondary Schools, Bible Clubs, Churches and Campus Fellowships to teach people, especially youths the Word of God and serves as a school text book in subjects relating to literature, music and other creative works.

FOUNDATION BIBLE CLUB A-Z STORY BOOK
ISBN: 978-49874-2-2 ISBN: 978-978-49874-2-4
Volume 1 With 26 Stories, 26 Bible Lessons, 26 Rhymes And 26 Songs For Book For Young Minds

An adage says, "a man who builds a house without building his child builds what the child will later sell." Proverbs 22:6 says, "train up a child in the way he should go: and when he is old, he will not depart from it." This book is an attempt to assist parents and teachers to meet up to the challenges that befall them in carrying out this important function in the light of the moral decadence that is prevailing all over the world.

The first edition of the book was used by several thousands of teachers, ministers and parents in schools, Churches and homes to build the moral values of young ones. Apart from the stories, songs and Bible passages for the young ones to study, there is a seminar material that is based on the lecture which the author delivered to school proprietors, children ministers and Christian professionals in this volume.

RANSOM FOR LOVE
ISBN: 978-49874-8-1 ISBN: 978-978-4987-4-8-6

She accepted his marriage proposal without knowing the kind of person he was. She soon discovered that he was a mean and ruthless guy who was always ready to get whatever he wanted by all means even if he has to pay for it with the lives of others. She was in his bondage, especially when her parents who believed he was a generous and gentleman were on his side.

Because she considered the proposal to marry him as a marriage engagement with the devil incarnate, she decided that she would rather die than to share her life with him. Then out of the blues, this passionate gentleman sneaked into her life despite all she did to discourage him. She could not resist his love for her when he offered to set her free from the devil incarnate. Then the battle began – sooner than they anticipated.

THE WEIGHT OF DEATH
ISBN: 9978-36348-0-1 ISBN: 978-978-36348-0-0
(Story Of The Spirit Eyes Series)

PLAY ONE: HORROR IN THE FAMILY: Talimi probably did not envisage his death when he was trying to compel his son, Damola to succeed him in the occult Brotherhood. Other members of the secret cult were aware of the battle between them. So when Talimi died; his family, especially Damola who was a diehard Christian began to fall prey to the cult. Using all their powers and the spirit that posed as Talimi's ghost, the cult waged war against the family, tormenting and making them to be at loggerheads.

PLAY TWO: RITUAL KIDS' KIDNAPPERS: Victor and the rest of the members of the School Bible Club were taught that there are lots of evil people in this world but he did not understand why God allowed him to be among the children that were taken away from their parents. He soon understood that he was to be used by God to rescue other children who did not know that everyone that truly believes in Jesus has the power to overcome evil.

PLAY THREE: THE WEIGHT OF DEATH: Awoseun would not have known the real source of problems of mankind if his father had not given him the power to see demons tormenting the people in different ways. What he was yet to know, however, was the power of light over darkness. When he was caught in crossfire between these powers, he desperately sought for deliverance.

FOOTSTEPS IN THE MUD
ISBN: 978-36348-9-5 ISBN: 978-978-36348-9-3

The Drama Package Of Results Of Research Works That trace Global And Societal Vices To The Corrupt Or Lost Of Family Values

The 13-Episode drama book involves Bosede who learnt many wrong things from her parents' conduct and foul language. She was forced to marry Kola when she became pregnant. Using her mother's method to handle her father, she tried to subject Kola to her control. In the course of that, she made life terrible for him. Although her mother tried to warn her of the implications of maltreating her husband but Bosede has grown out of control. Consequently, while looking for peace, Kola was pushed out of the house. He made friends with some guys who taught him the unholy ways of life and influenced him to become a menace in the house.

Junior who was born at time the couple never proved to be responsible parents also learnt wrong things from them. He decided to follow his father's footsteps by taking alcohol when he was in primary school. As if that was not bad enough, he tried to teach other children in the school the madness in his home. A school teacher, however, was able to influence him and his mother by teaching them Christian morals. Even then, Junior was soon caught in the crossfire at home as his father tried to enlist him as a future member of a secret cult that posed as a social club.

SUCCESSFUL CHRISTIANITY AND BASIC MINISTRIES
ISBN: 978-49874-6-0

A Collection Of Resource Materials That Precedes Christian Ministries And Basic Leadership Course Book

The first question is how Christianity is practiced even in a hostile environment. Next to that is the question about the potentials of Christians in spite of their apparent limitations. The other issues are connected to the successes, deliverance, callings, basic ministries of all Christians and evangelism. Various schools of thoughts have attempted these questions but many answers only portray Christianity as a form of religion instead of a way of life as specified by God. Some answers give room for compromise, hypocrisies, dogmas and denominational doctrines. The misconceptions about these areas of Christianity have brought about worldliness instead of righteousness and false achievements instead of fulfillment.

This book which contains six different subjects had been used to hold seminars at various levels, train ministers and Christian workers in Bible Schools and to equip the Church. It explains in simple terms the seemingly complex issues on practice of Christianity, Potentials, Deliverance, God's Kind Of Success, Evangelism and Basic Ministries of a Christian with Biblical principles, life transforming stories and illustrations.

CHRISTIAN MINISTRIES AND BASIC LEADERSHIP
ISBN: 978-36348-7-9 ISBN: 978-978-36348-7-9
A Collection Of Resource Materials That Follows Up Successful Christianity And Basic Ministries Course Book

As it is common to say that the hood does not make a monk, the dignified positions and bogus titles of many Christian leaders in modern days do not really make them Gospel Ministers.

This course book - a compilation of five resource materials on Missions And Outreach Ministries, Christian Communication Arts, Christian Leadership, Christian Education Methodology and Ministries Of Improvisations - aims at making every matured Christian an effective minister and leader at their respective homes, communities and nations. It teaches various ways Christians can communicate the word of God, meeting up to their responsibilities as ministers and leaders that reconcile people to God, edifying the Body Of Christ and reaching out to souls at the same time.

All of the resource materials are in use in Bible Schools like College Of Christian Education And Missions, in Churches and other ministries to raise Christian workers, Evangelists, Missionaries and other Ministers that serve at various levels and leadership capacities.

INSANITY OF HUMANITY
ISBN: 978-36348-6-0 ISBN: 978-978-36348-6-2
The Results Of Research Works Into Various Methods Of Brainwashing

Man is made to exercise his freewill. The mind of his own and the power to choose between right and wrong, good and evil, light and darkness is about to be washed away through brainwashing. The agents of control dubbed as Secret Government by John Todd (the top

Illuninati defector) have put necessary machinery in place to ensure that all human beings are in conformity in their thinking and ways of life, trying to wipe away diversity, which makes each person unique.

This book attempts to shed light on how the techniques of mind control are applied through the use of propaganda, education, entertainments, drugs, religions, media and other means of communications. It is the result of research works, some of which are based on findings of various researchers and writers like Bugger Lugz, Edward Hunter, Hadley Cantril, Herbert Krugman, David L. Robb, Vaughan Bell, Juliana Gomez, Ryan Duffy Vice, Henry Makow, David Nicholls, Fritz Springmeire, Steven Hassan, Renate Thienel, Debra Pursell, Mary Pride and a host of others who are acknowledged in this book.

CALVARY ROCK RESOURCE BOOKLETS
ISSN: 1595 93X

The Quarterly Missionary Booklets That Are Designed To Teach Children, Youths And Adults In Schools, Fellowships, Churches, At Homes, Office And Other Places.

Although all the various volumes of this booklet can be used independently of other books but it is recommended that it should be used as part of supplementary materials to make up for Foundation and Network Bible Club Story Books for both children and adults in School, Church, Campus, Office and other Fellowships.

Each of the volume is rich with quarterly Bible lessons, stories, drama, songs, seminar, tract materials and a host of other things that can be used to edify, educate, entertains and evangelize every category of people, ranging from children to elderly persons.

Every volume is designed to equip school teachers, ministers in Churches or campus or office fellowships and other people who wish to work with the Lord.

All These And Other Books Are Distributed Worldwide And Published By The Publishing House Of Calvary Rock Resources

*Ikenne-Remo, Nigeria
*Manchester, United Kingdom
*New York, United States

www.calvaryrock.org